*To Katherine and Rosemary.
A special thanks to my local Starbuck's for the coffee that kept me humming, and for the electricity that kept the laptop alive.*

"It only takes one match to ignite a haystack, or one remark to fire a mind."

LAWRENCE DURRELL

CONTENTS

Dedication	
Epigraph	
The Templar Map	1
Copyright	2
A Notice About Reviews:	3
Chapter 1	4
Chapter 2	9
CHAPTER 3	12
Chapter 4	16
Chapter 5	18
Chapter 6	21
Chapter 7	27
Chapter 8	30
Chapter 9	36
Chapter 10	42
Chapter 11	56
Chapter 12	60
Chapter 13	68
Chapter 14	77
Chapter 15	78

Chapter 16	89
Chapter 17	98
Chapter 18	102
Chapter 19	113
Chapter 20	122
Chapter 21	129
Chapter 22	135
Chapter 23	145
Chapter 24	156
Chapter 25	163
Chapter 26	169
Chapter 27	174
Reviews:	185

THE TEMPLAR MAP

Book 1

K.R. Hill

Copyright 2017
Kevin R. Hill,
Amazon Edition
All rights reserved. This book or parts thereof may not be reproduced in any form, stored in any retrieval system, or transmitted in any form by any means—electronic, mechanical, photocopy, recording, or otherwise—without prior written permission of the author, except as provided by United States of America copyright law.

The people in this book exist solely in the imagination of the author. Any resemblance to person or persons, living or dead, is a coincidence and not intended by the author.

Cover design: pro_ebookcovers

* * *

A NOTICE ABOUT REVIEWS:

Please take a few minutes to review this book on Amazon.

For writers like myself, getting your review means the world, even if that review is only a few words.

Thank you.

K.R.Hill

CHAPTER 1

Cologne, Germany

Uri turned the corner and noticed the tall white van parked with two of its wheels up on the curb. He touched his coat to make sure his weapon was there, stepped between the van and the car behind it, and reached for the rear door.

The instant he touched the handle, someone shoved a pistol against his neck.

"Who are you?" asked the gunman, and moved a scanner over Uri's hand. "Lieutenant Uri Dent," he read. "I am sorry. They are waiting for you."

Uri climbed inside and sat on a bench with three men. The four of them jumped to their feet and saluted when the gray-haired man in the passenger seat turned.

"At ease," he said, motioning the group to sit. He was in his sixties, with deep lines on his face, a well-trimmed, sharp line mustache, and shoulder length hair that hung around a stern face.

"Men," continued the older man. "I hand-picked you for this mission. You are the Vatican's best. We take our orders from his Eminence himself—no other. An artifact stolen from the Vatican has surfaced. Our mission is to capture and return it. We traced it here, to Cologne. The man carrying it is Yosef Jobani. He's in the bar to our right and should have it with him."

He showed them a tablet. On the screen was the image of a rectangular, metal object, covered with strange writing.

"What is it?" asked one of the men.

"It is Solomon's Key."

The men looked at one another.

"That's a children's story about treasure."

"This is no myth, gentlemen. Excavated beneath Solomon's temple in 1129 by the Knights Templar, and acquired by Pope Honorius II, it was Vatican property for two hundred years. A priest, made bold by Martin Luther, smuggled it out of St. Peter's during construction. It disappeared until now."

"What sort of metal–"

"Listen!" snapped the commander. "Our Scholars believe it is a map to Solomon's mines, and the greatest treasure the world has ever seen. We are to secure it by any means. Do you understand?"

"Yes sir," said the men, almost in unison.

The commander sorted through a folder and removed a photo. "This is the target, Dr. Yosef Jobani. We believe he is meeting a buyer. Here is the layout of the bar."

The old man unbuttoned his coat. "Our intel says you have four minutes before the exchange. We can't risk the Key getting away. Go!"

A light rain touched the back of Uri's neck as climbed from the van. The other men hurried to the bar. One of them bumped him and said, "He's sitting in the far corner with two bodyguards. The place is packed with people."

A group of students stepped out of the bar laughing. One of them was singing loudly.

"Okay, men," said Uri. "Two minutes and fifty-nine seconds. I'm taking point." He touched the knife on his belt.

The men checked their weapons and nodded approval.

"You," snapped Uri to one of the men. "You're at the back door. No one comes out."

"No one," agreed the thin-faced man. He pulled on a black beanie and rushed away.

Uri tapped an index finger against the chest of one of the other men. "You. You're backup at the front door. If I fail, you stop the guy. The commander said do what it takes. You know what that means."

"It means war." The man removed his weapon from a pocket, pulled back the action and let it snap back into place, injecting a bullet into the firing chamber.

* * *

In a corner booth sat the man he was looking for, a young Egyptian with a beard, a Palestinian scarf around his neck.

The man looked right and left and tried to stand. One of his no-neck bodyguards shoved him into the seat.

The instant Uri moved into view, one of the bodyguards saw him, shouted and jumped to his feet. Uri launched himself forward, but the bodyguard blocked his punches and wrapped him in a headlock. Then the other bodyguard attacked.

Uri fought to reach his knife. Several blows landed on his face and chest. Then he found the knife and stabbed the man who was holding him in the thigh. With a shout, the bleeding man leaned sideways, and that small shift of weight was all Uri needed. He moved a few inches and shoved the knife into the man's side, twisting the blade between the bodyguard's ribs, tearing them apart.

The grip around his neck went slack. The man holding him dropped to the floor.

"The item is on the move," shouted Uri, as Jobani climbed onto his seat and stepped onto the table, kicked beer glasses and ash trays out of his way, and leaped to the next table.

"Gun!" shouted a bar patron.

The students crowding the floor moved as one toward the exit.

"Gun, gun," shouted several drinkers as they pushed through

the crowd jamming the exit. Beer glasses shattered on the floor. Customers pushed over tables and tried to jump over the crowd at the door. Men shouted. Women screamed.

Uri followed Jobani while still fighting the second bodyguard, a trained boxer. He was all punches, rapid flurries of jabs and hooks. His punches knocked Uri back. Blood flowed into Uri's eyes, and he kept wiping them to clear his vision. Through the blur he saw the guy with Solomon's Key climbing to his feet near the exit. He screamed, "Backup, get the package!"

Uri fought and punched, tried to sweep the boxer's leg with a kick to his knee, but nothing stopped the guy. Then he used his last move. Uri dropped to his knees and lunged forward, getting beneath the boxer's defenses, and slashed his thigh, severing the femoral artery. The man punched a few more times, but the punches were weak, as though the boxer's batteries were dead.

Uri ran to the exit.

Jobani tried to fight, but was not trained. There was no power in his swings. In fifteen seconds Uri had him against a table, a knife pressed under his chin.

"Did you get it?" One of Uri's men shouted.

Jobani stopped fighting. "You'll never get it," he laughed, shaking his head from side to side.

"Where is it? Tell me or die." Uri pressed the knife against the professor's throat so hard that it cut the skin, and blood ran down his neck.

"It is gone. Your Vatican will never have it."

Uri searched Jobani, then looked on the seat where he had been sitting, and beneath the table.

"Did it get past you?" Uri asked the agent at the door.

"I don't know. I can't check everyone. Fuck!" The man kicked the bar.

The professor rolled off the table onto the floor, and jumped up with a jagged beer glass.

Uri slit his throat and wiped the knife across the professor's chest as an afterthought, turned and walked into the falling rain.

* * *

The windshield wipers slapped up and down as the engine started and the lights came on. Uri climbed inside the van and sat down.

"Where is number four?" asked the commander, turning in the passenger seat. "Did we lose a man?"

One of the men spoke. "He was taken. A group of Brits, some kind of sports team, must've seen his weapon and attacked him. They were calling the police when I passed."

"You allowed one of my men to be taken into custody?" The commander didn't miss a beat. He raised his weapon and shot the offender in the chest. The man slumped sideways and fell against Uri's feet.

"That means we're compromised." The commander opened an envelope and pulled out several passports, opened each one, looked at the photograph, and handed it to the correct man. "Get rid of your weapons and everything connected with this operation. Get out of Germany today. Follow protocol. While you were inside, we got word that Jobani visited a symposium of archeologists. He may have passed the Key to one of the American professors."

"So," said Uri, "what now?"

"We are going to the United States. We'll search through the data, analyze video footage, and track the professors. If one of them has it, we'll find him."

CHAPTER 2
Two months later, Long Beach, California

"DeMontey?" Jason Dalton walked up the stairs and onto the old marble landing. "You coming to my class this afternoon?"

Three black school kids stopped in the corridor and pulled up their baggy pants and looked Dalton up and down. One of them twisted his cap around so the brim was over the side of his face.

"Momma say don't talk to no white police." DeMontey slung his pack over a shoulder and motioned with a nod for his buddies to continue walking.

"I'm not a cop." Dalton pointed to his office door. "You see there," he said, underlining one of the words on the glass, "that says *Private* detective. That means your momma can come and pay me to find you. The police work for the city. I work for the people."

DeMontey marched over. "If I come, you gunna teach me to fight the way you did wit' my momma's friend when you mashed his head into the wall?"

"Yes."

"Will you ask Momma if I can come?"

"Yes."

The boys pushed and laughed as they hurried past, hopping and jumping down the stairs. Dalton chuckled and watched them for a moment, then pushed open his office door and walked in.

"Hey, hold this thing, would you?" asked Nick, standing on a ladder, shoving a bubble surveillance camera into a hole in the ceiling. Bits of plaster speckled Nick's red hair and the carpet. A drill sat on the old librarian desk. "Take that shovel and hold it."

Dalton picked up the shovel that was leaning against the wall, and pressed the handle against the bubble.

The ladder creaked as Nick shifted his stance. "Okay, it should stay now, if you don't move. Hold still."

"Do you know what you're doing?"

"If you'd stop moving, it might stay."

"We can't pay the electric bill, but you had to go and buy a camera?"

Nick batted the handle out of the way and hurried down the ladder. "I got it at Costco for $29.99. Wanna know why I bought it?"

"Yes." Dalton set the shovel down and took off his jacket and threw it over the back of the wooden chair, pulled off his shoulder holster, and placed it in the bottom drawer of the old desk.

"Because of these." Nick tucked his red hair over one ear, and held up a glass of water.

"Is that ...." Dalton took the glass and held it up in the sunlight that flooded the office through the window.

"Two bugs; one's a listening device. The other one's a tracker. That's what scares me: That tracker has a limited range, so whoever's after you is close. You been messing with any married women?"

Dalton set the glass on the desk and dropped into the chair.

"Is there a case you're not telling me about?" said Nick.

"No, nothing."

"Look, I'm just the computer geek, but some of the people we investigate kill people. I need to know what's going on so I don't get shot." Nick grabbed the edge of the desk.

"I don't know where those bugs came from."

"Boss, if you're working a case without–"

"I'm not. If I was taking more cases, we wouldn't be in this dump building."

A knock made Dalton look up. Two figures moved about outside the opaque glass door. He pulled his gun from the drawer.

CHAPTER 3

Uri Dent gripped the knife as he crept along the alley. The falling snow of Chicago collected on his lashes and pricked his scalp like tiny needles.

At a warped and peeling door, he sucked in a deep breath and swept his gaze over apartment windows. He turned right, then left. From his pocket he removed a pair of surgical gloves. They made rubbery sounds as he pulled them on.

"In and out in ten minutes," said the commander. "Find out if he has the Key. It has to be this Professor Urtsen."

Uri shut off the phone in his ear with a tap of his finger, and slowly turned the doorknob. When the latch clicked, he opened the door three inches, grabbed the warning bell, and entered the hallway, crouching and staring into the darkness, his pulse a drum-beat in his head.

Down the hallway he saw a muslin curtain. From the other side of the curtain, he heard a man's voice. A woman answered and giggled. Uri paused and shook his head, took out a photograph from his shirt pocket, looked through the curtain to verify that the man on the bed was the man in the photograph.

And then he heard a growl, deep and vicious.

He gasped and seized the knife, grinding his teeth and panting. His knife hand shook from side to side.

With lowered head, the Great Dane moved into view, ears back, fangs exposed, eyes flashing. Its legs quivered as it turned its head, about to leap.

Uri jumped back and flinched, ready for the pain and blood, ready for those massive jaws to clamp down on his leg and shred the flesh. But instead of attacking, the animal whined, and he knew it was not fully grown. The puppy in it wanted to play.

He almost dropped to the floor, holding his body upright with a hand on his knee, shaking his head. After a moment, Uri wiped sweat from his brow and held out his hand.

"Come on, big dog," he whispered, led the dog to the bathroom and closed it inside.

His eyes never moved from the curtain in the doorway ahead. Two yards from it, he heard feminine yelping noises and moved the tips of his shoes to within an inch of the fabric. The white muslin rippled as he leaned close.

Across the room stood a four-poster bed. A young blond woman, wearing a leather corset and fishnet stockings, smiled and strained in the fur-covered hand cuffs that held her bent over the bed.

"Oh, Daddy, hurry back and give it to me," pleaded the woman, rolling her head about.

Through a doorway across the room, a shadow moved about. Now was Uri's chance. He could get in and get past the woman without the man being alerted.

Uri rushed through the curtain. He didn't get more than a foot before he heard the popping, crackling sound of a stun gun.

He felt a red-hot sword shoved into his brain.

※ ※ ※

He woke to voices in a fog.

"Oh Daddy, feel his muscles," said the woman, balancing on her knees while clamping his wrist to the headboard with handcuffs.

"Should I zap him again, baby?" asked Prof. Urtsen.

"Oh no, let him wake up. We're going to have fun with this one." The woman opened his belt.

Uri didn't have time to think. He had to get his body working and moving. If the woman got handcuffs on his other wrist, he might be kept here for days. With all the force left in his body, he twisted at the waist and kicked. His shin connected with the woman's neck and knocked her against the wall. She crashed to the floor with a shriek.

But he couldn't be happy with that. He had to move again. Only one of the threats had been neutralized. The second one was coming around the bed with that crackling stun gun in his hand.

Uri rolled off the edge of the bed and tugged on the handcuff again and again, jerking the bed about the floor, lifting it off the carpet. He pulled and jerked and shouted. Saliva shot out of his mouth.

The maniac with the stun gun was almost on him when a section of the headboard broke loose. Uri shoved it at the professor.

The old professor tried to reach Uri with the gun, but he couldn't.

Uri ran at him, using the headboard like a battering ram, and shoved him against the wall.

The professor struggled until Uri knocked him out.

Now that Uri was safe, he dropped to the bed. He tried to wipe his face and realized his hand was still handcuffed to the broken headboard. So, he stood up and smashed the headboard against a table. On the third swing it broke apart and he was free, a furry hand cuff clamped to his wrist. As he searched the room, he saw the earbud on the bedside table and noticed a blinking red light.

He shoved the device into his ear and turned it on.

"Uri?" said the commander. "The key has surfaced in Los Angeles. Get out of there and get on a plane."

"What should I do with these perverts?"

"Where are they?"

"Passed out."
"Sounds like you had a good time."
Uri turned off the phone.

CHAPTER 4

"That must be the Switzers." Nick hurried to the second-hand filing cabinets and took a clipboard and his cell phone from a top drawer. "Yeah, three o'clock, they're right on time."

Dalton hurried to let his clients in.

"Here's the file." Nick handed his boss a large brown envelope and tapped it several times. "The case is closed, so get the check," he whispered. "Full payment, no installments. One big fat check."

Nick opened the door and greeted the elderly couple.

Mrs. Switzer held her husband's shaking hand and led him across the office.

It didn't take long for Dalton to explain the investigation and present the evidence to the elderly couple.

Mrs. Switzer gasped and held one of the photos to her chest. "Harry, look, it's Lauren." Then she turned to Dalton. "She started getting in trouble with the wrong crowd, and about a year later she just disappeared. We thought we lost her, Mr. Dalton."

"You didn't lose her. In fact, this is her address and phone number. We spoke to her, and she is looking forward to seeing you."

Mrs. Switzer clutched a handkerchief tightly to her mouth and sobbed. "Harry, we have a granddaughter!"

"Her name is Helen."

After much talk, Mrs. Switzer asked her husband to write a check, but while he was writing it, she touched his arm. "On second thought, dear, let me write it. I want to give Mr. Dalton a nice bonus."

Over at the door, where the couple could not see him, Nick danced as though he'd walked into a Mardi Gras parade.

"Well, thank you so much." Dalton took the check and set it on the corner of the desk. "We are happy to have been of service." He walked over and helped the couple to their feet, held Mrs. Switzer's arm, and led her to the door.

Nick was sniffing the check by the time Dalton closed the door.

"Oh, the smell of money. I'd forgotten that smell."

"Now you can buy some glue to hold your cheapo camera in the ceiling."

"Fire-power is what we need. Did you figure out who planted those surveillance devices?"

"Are you on that again?" Dalton walked to the desk.

"If you don't tell me, I'm going to find another job."

"Yeah, you can go back to building fake backgrounds."

Nick slammed a filing cabinet drawer. "Let's get one thing clear: you didn't catch me."

"No, but when one of your good fella's clients decided you knew too much, you came to me for help."

"Do you have to remind me again?"

"And you stopped that. You work for me now. Say it." Dalton pointed.

"I work for you now. I don't help criminals anymore."

"You better not."

"Don't you have that karate class today?"

CHAPTER 5

The black Lincoln rolled to a stop in the parking lot. The chain-link fence that bordered the lot was rusted and cut in places. The wind blew a red candy wrapper into a patch of dead grass. For several minutes the car stood still, gray exhaust rising into the cold morning air.

The driver, Samoan tattoos on his tree-trunk neck, climbed out and opened the rear door. From the back seat, a man in his sixties placed a polished black shoe on the ground. Bits of glass crunched beneath his shoes as he stood.

"Sir, do you want to take my weapon?"

"No, James," answered the elderly man, brushing a speck from his black overcoat. "I have Sadie with me."

"Sadie, Sir?"

The older man pulled off a red leather glove and took a stub-nose revolver from his pocket. He smiled. "This is Sadie. Watch my six."

The chauffer nodded approval. "I always watch your back, Sir."

The two crossed the parking lot to a large truck parked parallel to the street. The sign on its side read BISHOP'S PLUMBING: THE FAMILY PLUMBER.

"James, stay here, but be ready. This could get ugly, so keep the engine running."

James opened the back door of the plumbing truck, and

Thomas Trenton Gregory climbed in and closed the door.

The truck smelled of cigarettes and sweat. "Gentlemen," said Mr. Gregory, nodding at two men seated behind a small table. He also greeted Jeremy, a long-haired young man with rounded shoulders and a pot belly, who sat in front of a console of electrical equipment, a brown knit cap holding back his hair.

Mr. Gregory sat at the table. "Your commanding officer spoke highly of you. You were good soldiers. I need a simple extraction. You pick up the package, drop him off, and job done."

Jeremy stopped cleaning his glasses and tapped a monitor. "That's the package there. His name is Jason Dalton. He's the guy teaching the class."

One of the men shoved his sleeves up his forearms, revealing a Ranger tatt on one arm. "Permission to speak, Sir."

Mr. Gregory twisted off the cap of a silver Thermos, and poured coffee. "Speak."

"The guy is teaching karate to children." He pointed, looked at the other men in the van, and laughed. "Let's just walk over and snatch him. How hard can that be?"

The man laughed again and reached into his jacket pocket. His laughter stopped abruptly though, when he saw a revolver cocked to fire.

The instant Mr. Gregory aimed the revolver, Jeremy jumped from his seat and shoved a sawed-off shotgun against Mr. Tattoo's face.

"Whoa, whoa, whoa," said the other man, throwing up his hands. "Everyone, slow and easy, let's put the guns down."

"That's a twelve-gauge in your face," said Mr. Gregory, clicking his tongue as a parent would to scold a toddler. "You reached into a pocket. I hope there is not a weapon in there. That would make Jeremy here nervous. It's all those energy drinks. The last time he pulled that cannon, his hands were shaking so badly he tapped the trigger by accident. What a mess, clumps of hair and brain stuck to the walls." He shook his head, but the revolver did not move.

The man with the tattoo raised his hands and set them on

the table.

"Good choice," said Jeremy with a sigh, lowering the shotgun. "I hate cleaning up; puts me off sushi for months."

"Okay," Gregory nodded and clicked the revolver's firing pin to its safe position. "Back to business. Now, this is my money, and I don't want to waste it. That man you see teaching children has taught hand-to-hand in military facilities that Congress doesn't know about. If you underestimate him, he'll put you down, and I'll be out my money. I don't like to waste money. Are we clear?"

"Yes, sir."

"Good." Gregory set the revolver on the table. "This is his file." He shoved a folder across the table.

The men read and passed photos between them. "Why all the blacked-out pages?" one asked.

"He ran a black-on-black squad for Uncle Sam. Only the top brass see his unedited file."

One of them pointed to the man on the screen. "He's got more medals than-"

"Is there a problem, gentlemen?" Mr. Gregory placed his hand on the revolver.

Jeremy raised the shotgun.

"Transport him alive to the drop. This is half your payment. I'll pay the other fifty percent on delivery." Mr. Gregory reached into his coat and set a leather satchel on the table.

One of the men unzipped it and spread the opening wide, revealing the contents to the man beside him. "We're good," he said.

Mr. Gregory stood up. "Then until this evening, gentlemen. You walk into his office at seventeen-hundred hours, and should be at the drop by eighteen-thirty."

CHAPTER 6

Dalton opened a gold envelope and pulled out a card. "It's a thank-you from the Switzers."

"I wish we'd get more bonuses like that," laughed Nick.

"Man, this heat. I have to get some air." Dalton tugged on the window, thumped the top edge with a fist, and tugged again. "I'm going to get a crowbar and–" He watched a Bentley pull to the curb in the street below. "Now that's money." He whistled.

Nick rushed over and looked. "The driver checked our address. He's coming up here, rich people with chauffeurs and expensive shoes. Oh, yeah, more money is coming our way. Quick, clean the office."

Dalton sat at the desk and took the glass of water with the listening devices in it, and shoved it into a drawer. He was gathering up papers and shoving them into drawers, when he heard high heels clicking on the landing. That sound took his memory on roller coaster ride of bedroom scenes. He held his breath as she crossed the room. And of course he remembered Jax, the woman he spoke to when he was alone and drinking bourbon.

"I'm looking for—the sign on the door, it says J. Dalton, Private Detective."

Dalton looked her over, from the Italian kitten heels, to a neck line low enough to be intriguing. He didn't know what to call the tight white dress or the distorted checkerboard pattern of the blouse, but he knew he liked it.

"I'm Jason Dalton." He stood and reached for her hand. "This is my assistant, Nick. Please, have a seat. How can I help?"

"Nice to meet you. I'm Sophie Devonshire." She touched the pearls around her neck and glanced at Nick.

"Nick," said Dalton. "Can you wait in the other room?"

When the door closed, Sophie Devonshire slid forward and lowered her head as though summoning courage. "I have a delicate matter that I need help with."

He looked up the moment she stopped speaking, and walked around the desk and sat beside her. "I'm sworn to secrecy. What can I help with?"

"I was going through my late husband's things, and came across a curious artifact." She reached into her bag and took out what looked like an old piece of metal, the size of a paperback novel. Strange writing covered one side. "As soon as I began making inquiries, bad things started happening." She glanced over her shoulder, touched the neckline of her blouse, and pulled the fabric together.

"First of all, Mrs. Devonshire, why'd you come to me?"

"Oh—" She stared for a moment. "Yes, well, I came to you because a few months ago I was on a business trip to DC. I was at a political fund-raiser, and met a mysterious army officer. We chatted, and he recommended you."

"A black man?"

"Excuse me?" she asked.

"African-American? Was the officer you spoke to a black man?"

"Yes, he was."

"Okay, Mrs. Devonshire, I know who that was. We served together. So, getting back to what you were saying, you mentioned that some bad things had happened when you tried to find out what this was. Define bad things." Dalton examined the object.

"Before I say another word, I wish to retain your services. That way everything I say stays private. Is that the way it works?"

She set a thick envelope on the desk. "Will this serve as a retainer?"

Dalton opened the envelope and saw the bills were all hundreds; he guessed there was ten thousand dollars there. "That will be fine, Mrs. Devonshire."

"Please, Sophie is my name. I had a break-in at the house. Two men have threatened my attorney and demanded money to settle my husband's bills, but refused to show records of any kind. And two days ago, a man tried to steal my purse. Another man threatened me in public and demanded I turn over the artifact. I assumed he was talking about that."

Dalton scratched the object with a letter opener. "It's plaster, he said, rubbing some of the crumbs between thumb and finger."

"I don't understand. If it's plaster, then why all the fuss? Oh, I forgot. These were taped to it." She handed him a thumb drive and a small glass vial with a few granules inside. "There's a photo of that thing on the thumb drive."

Dalton took the items and tapped the vial. "Maybe the photo is the real deal, and the vial holds scrapings to authenticate."

She opened her handbag and took out a silver cigarette case, removed one, tapped it on the case several times, and lit it. "My husband was a respected archaeologist, but he may have been involved in some dubious affairs. I need you to be a buffer between me and those terrible men. Can you find out what Andrew was involved in?"

"I need your attorney's card, and the location where they tried to take your purse."

"These are the cards you need." Sophie leaned forward and placed the cards on the desk. "That other card is my bank. I was coming down the steps when a man grabbed my purse."

"And he took it?"

She smiled and her eyes brightened. "Not hardly, Mr. Dalton. I was raised in Texas. It'd take more than a punk in a hoodie to get my bag."

Dalton leaned back and nodded. "Good. I like it. You should

be–"

There was a noise on the landing, and Dalton reached for his gun. As he opened the drawer he glanced at the clock. The hour hand moved to five-o'clock.

"Oh." Sophie slid forward on the wooden chair and turned. "That must be my driver. Don't be alarmed. Mr. Abbyton, I won't be long."

A figure moved in front of the glass door, and it opened quickly. A man in military black rushed into the room and knelt, pointing a short assault rifle. "Clear," he barked, and another man ran into the office.

Nick walked in the side door, and one of the commandos shot him.

The force of the shot threw Nick against the wall, and he crashed to the floor.

Sophie Devonshire screamed and ran into the corner, dropped to her knees and covered her head.

Dalton grabbed the shovel and stood before her, ready to fight.

The second guy discharged his weapon.

White pain shot like a skyrocket through Dalton's brain, and he doubled over. After the initial flash and shock, he realized he wasn't bleeding or dying, and knew they were firing bean bag ammo.

The soldier who'd shot Nick jerked his weapon. "Someone wants to talk with you. Either you come standing up, or we carry you." He discharged his weapon and hit Dalton in the thigh.

This time the shot hit bone, and Dalton cried out and used the shovel to keep himself standing.

He hobbled forward and was about to swing the shovel, when the report of a handgun, so different from the hollow boom sound the assault rifles made, drew Dalton's attention to the door.

Into the office ran a huge man with a bald head, holding a revolver with both hands, jerking it about. He fired twice, two head shots, and the commandos fell.

Sophie Devonshire ran and tried to reach the artifact on the desk, but Dalton lunged and got in front of her, and pushed her to the corner.

The bald guy leaned forward and said: "It's not here. I don't see it." He tapped the device in his ear and jerked his weapon about as though moving behind enemy lines. For a second he looked at Sophie and Dalton, and fired again.

Dalton jerked the shovel to his face. The bullet hit and ricocheted through the window.

"The time is up," shouted someone from the landing. "Get out!"

Before the killer fired another round, he saw the artifact on the desk, rushed over and grabbed it, and ran toward the door.

He nearly made it.

Nick had inched his way to one of the assault rifles. When the killer turned and ran, Nick grabbed the weapon and fired twice, hitting the guy on the arm and hip.

The killer doubled over and barked as he ran from the office.

"Hey, are you okay?" Dalton groaned, leaned over, and touched Nick's shoulder.

"What the hell just happened?"

"Is that camera thing you stuck in the ceiling recording?" asked Dalton, looking about the office. "The police will be here soon. Take the cash and Mrs. Devonshire and the surveillance, and get out of here."

Nick wheezed, climbed to his feet, groaned, and touched his chest.

"They were firing bean bags. That's why we're not dead."

"Damn, I got kicked by a mule," said Nick.

"That mule got us both." In the distance a siren screamed. Dalton motioned with his chin. "That's got to be for us."

"I didn't call it in."

"Someone did. Get Mrs. Devonshire safe at home, drop the cash and go to the diner. Remember the code-red diner I told you about?"

Nick nodded. "Seal Beach, beside the jetty, right? Do I get a gun? Did you see me nail that fucker?"

"You were shooting bean bags. You're lucky the guy didn't pop your head. Go now. I'll meet you when the police are finished. Make sure you're not followed. Just like I taught you." He handed the particle sample to Nick, but let him tug before he released it.

"I won't lose it, boss."

He grabbed Nick's arm. "Whoever sent the soldiers is still out there. Don't let him find you."

"They're the ones tracking you, right?"

"We're sure as hell going to find out."

Nick pivoted from right to left as though trying to decide which way to run, then jumped forward, hurried back into the office and grabbed Sophie Devonshire's hand, and pulled her out the door.

"Take my car," she said, trying to run in heels.

CHAPTER 7

The two patrolmen came up the stairs with weapons drawn, backs pressed against the wall, and shouted into the office.

"I'm here. I'm Jason Dalton."

The cops peeked around the doorway and entered quickly, one after the other, one pointing his weapon right, the other left. When they saw the bodies, their guns turned to Dalton.

"Easy guys, I'm a PI. I have a license. My weapon is in the drawer." Dalton sat at the desk with his hands clasped together behind his head, and motioned to the drawer with an elbow.

"What happened?" asked one of the patrolmen.

"I've been told not to say anything until my attorney arrives."

"You think that'll look good for you, you lawyering up so quick like that? Go stand in the corner." The heavy-set, older cop holstered his weapon, pulled a latex glove from his pocket, and opened the desk. He reached in and lifted the weapon, held it to his nose, and sniffed.

"Fired?" asked the other cop.

"No." The first one set the weapon down and walked to the commandos. "Each one was a head shot. Looks like a small-caliber weapon." He raised his voice and asked, "You own any other weapons, Mr. Dalton?"

"Ask my lawyer."

The heavy cop stood up and looked at Dalton. "What are you

trying to hide with your lawyer?"

"I'm trying to avoid being an easy target."

"Son-of-a-bitch," mumbled the heavy cop, adjusting the gear on his belt and walking toward Dalton.

"Back it up, Chauncey!" shouted his partner. "Everything's on camera now, remember?" His partner tapped the camera on his vest.

* * *

Mrs. Devonshire's attorney met Dalton at the police station. Every question the police asked got filtered through the lawyer, and he was released in two hours.

As Dalton was pulling on his jacket, preparing to leave, a tall, fat man approached.

"That deli makes the best brisket in SoCal." The fat man shoved the last of a sandwich into his mouth and brushed some crumbs from an overcoat. "Oh. Unbelievable." He chewed with bulging red cheeks.

Dalton tried to move past, but the guy blocked his path.

"Who are you?" Dalton demanded.

The fat man wagged a finger. "Oh, excuse me. Harvey Lowenthal. Special Agent Lowenthal. FBI, Art Theft Unit. I've been on the trail of a black-market antiquities ring for two years. Two days ago, I got a tip that this man entered the country." He opened a black folder and held up a photo.

The guy looked ten years younger and still had a bit of hair up top, but Dalton recognized the man that had killed two men in his office. He returned the photo. "Mister, I don't know you from Adam."

"Do you recognize this?" The fat man opened his identification.

Dalton took it and weighed the badge and said: "That guy in your photo left two bodies in my office. Each kill was a head shot, small-caliber revolver. That sound familiar?"

"Very. His name is Uri Dent. He's a killer."

"Good luck with that." Dalton stepped around.

Special agent Lowenthal shoved a night stick against Dalton's chest. "I'm out of patience, so why don't you—"

Dalton ripped the night stick out of the man's grasp. "I'm a private citizen and you just assaulted me, Special Agent. I'm sure there's cameras here that caught the entire thing. My attorney would love to see the footage." He dropped the stick on the floor.

The agent smiled. "I needed your prints. Looks like I've got them now." He bent over with a sigh and picked up the nightstick. "Your history came back sketchy. False identities look sketchy like that. Now I can check."

"You want my help, and you threaten me?" Dalton shook his head.

"Listen, Uri is on your trail. He's a person of interest in seven murders. They call him the Snake. The victims never see him coming. You should see what he did to a professor in Chicago."

"I need to get to my client."

"What does your client have, Dalton? What is valuable enough to make Uri enter the US?"

"I don't like you."

"Listen, asshole," said Lowenthal. "The feeling's mutual. If Uri is on your trail, you're going to need my help soon enough. When you do, call this number." He reached beneath a knit scarf and took out a business card.

Dalton flipped a thumb across a missing corner. "What happened to this? Did you get hungry?"

"I needed a toothpick."

Dalton tossed the card to the floor and walked away.

"We're going to talk again," called the agent. "Count on that."

CHAPTER 8

Wong's sat in the sand between two groups of palm trees. The restaurant was nothing more than a trailer covered with 1950s beige paint that left a milky residue on your pants when you brushed against it. The locals loved the diner because it reminded them of a simpler time. They could sit at the bar and look out and see nothing but beach and parking lot, and that made them feel as though they had escaped the city. It was the best thing about Wong's, and it wasn't even on the menu.

A misty rain began falling as Dalton crossed the parking lot. The mist turned into droplets when he was twenty feet from the diner. As he opened the front door of Wong's, he heard the rain tapping on the tin roof.

Toward the rear of the diner he saw Nick in one of the booths. He hurried through the restaurant and stepped out the back door.

After a few minutes, Nick walked onto the back porch with a glass of water in his hand.

"I'm glad you remembered this place," said Dalton.

"Don't say a word. Give me your phone." Nick grabbed Dalton's cell and dropped it into the water then pushed it down with his fingers. Water spilled on his shoes. "Hey, don't look at me like that. Those guys that stormed the office were not playing around. We don't know what kind of electronic gear they have."

"Oh, man." Dalton touched the glass. "No, you're right, but it's hard."

"Come on, I got the information you wanted."

They sat in a corner booth that felt sticky here and there. A young Asian girl with bright eyes and long black hair typed their order on an iPad, and hurried away. A moment later, she came back with a pot of coffee, set two cups on the table, and filled them.

Dalton watched her walk away. "Is Sophie Devonshire safe?" he asked.

"Yes. I dropped her at her house."

"Good. But that attack wasn't all about the case. Those first two guys were after me. They were military."

"Yeah, no shit. And I got something special if they send more people." Nick set a folded newspaper on the table. He looked around and unfolded it, revealing an army .45. "My daddy fought with that in Vietnam. Next time I won't be shooting bean bags."

"You don't have a permit to carry that thing. Have you ever fired a .45? You'll probably blow your own foot off." Dalton chuckled.

"Well, I guess we'll see."

"This case is sizzling. The bald guy, he was a pro. Did you see the way he handled himself?"

"Why didn't you tell me you were some kind of military hitman?"

For a moment Dalton didn't move. Then he said, "Ah, the computer whiz has been digging."

"I got shot. I saw two murders. You're damn right I did some digging."

"My unit had a security breech. I chose to protect my family by playing dead. The DOD gave me a new identity."

"And that woman?"

Dalton sat his coffee cup down hard. "Now you're getting personal. You're enjoying this."

"A lot." Nick smiled and leaned over the table.

"Is there anything you can't find on that damn computer?"

"Nothing."

"Asshole."

"Yep. Her name was all over your military records. That base, what's the name of it? You two lived together there. Who is Jax?"

Dalton looked at the ceiling. "We met when we were fifteen. She was— She was like a song that made me feel good. I don't know how else to say it."

"What happened?"

"That breach happened. We'd been taking out top cartel members in South America. Then two members of my unit got murdered. I had to decide if I wanted to put Jax in harm's way, and constantly worry about when one of the cartel men would find her. I chose to die and vanish. If I was dead, she'd be safe. The DOD set it up."

"So, you died and got a new identity."

"Yes. Now tell me about the case. Or is there more private stuff you want to ask me?"

"Man, I wish there was."

Nick took two envelopes from the booth and dropped them on the table. From one he pulled some papers. "Sophie Devonshire: she seems pretty legit. Her family is old money, married into it. Her husband was an archaeologist of some renown, wrote a couple books. Everything seems to check out." Nick waved a hand over the papers.

"What about the artifact?"

Nick nodded about six times, as though he'd had too much caffeine, picked up the second envelope and opened it. "This is where it goes sideways. I searched all over the net."

"Why are you so excited?"

"Because this artifact thing is freaking hot. I sent a notice to some PhD guy on a forum, and people were tracking me down within a minute. Hell, I was on a library computer, and they still got my phone number. That means major resources." Nick leaned over the table, his chin six inches above it. "Someone is spending a lot of time and money to find that thing."

"When Sophie Devonshire was in the office, remember what

she said?"

"She found it among her husband's things."

"She tried to find out what it was, and got threatened and robbed. Someone wants it badly." Dalton snapped back in his seat, pulled out his automatic and ejected the clip, and counted the bullets. "Get your gun!"

"Now?" Nick knocked over his cup and looked around, tried to jump out of his seat but hit the table and dropped onto his butt. He pointed the .45 here and there.

"Keep it under the table. That back door just opened four inches and closed." Dalton searched the diner. At the counter sat a guy slurping soup. His hair stuck out straight like it hadn't been brushed in days. Two stools down from the hair guy sat a fat man in shorts. His puffy pink legs made Dalton look away.

And then, out across the parking lot, he saw the vehicle that he didn't want to see: a black Porsche SUV crossing the lot with its lights turned off. It parked facing the diner.

"Is that .45 loaded?"

Nick's eyes got big. "Oh, hell, yes it's loaded. I got four extra clips too. The .45 is about to win the West again."

"I'm going to pretend you didn't say that."

Nick wobbled his head about like he was all embarrassed and shoved his hair back over an ear with the muzzle of the pistol.

"Holy crap! You're going to blow your ear off. Keep that thing down," said Dalton, rocking on his elbows. "Are you ready for this?"

"That won't happen again, boss. I'm sorry."

Two more black SUVs rolled into the parking lot and moved into position facing the diner.

"Those SUVs are cutting off our escape route," said Dalton. "I need you to take the guy at the back door. If he raises a weapon, you shoot to kill. Got it? It's the guy you shoot in the leg that kills you."

Dalton slid out of the booth, pulled off his jacket and covered his weapon. As he climbed to his feet the front door opened and an attractive woman walked in.

She stood five foot eight, Dalton guessed, and weighed 110 pounds. She had short black hair that almost touched her pinstripe jacket. In one ear sat a microphone with a curly wire that disappeared beneath her collar.

"Oh, the rain. I got wet," she said, and slowly removed her jacket. She nodded to Dalton and turned in a circle, holding her arms up. Then she walked to the wall and hung her jacket on a hook.

As she approached, he backed up a few steps and allowed her to sit at the booth.

"Let's sit down and have a little talk, shall we?" The woman patted the table top and pointed a finger at the seat across from her.

"You're not a cop or the FBI. I would've seen a badge by now if you were. That means you're on the other side of the line. And I'm guessing the men in those SUVs have their fingers on some high-dollar weapons."

Through the pass-through window into the kitchen, where Mr. and Mrs. Wong set the plates of food so their daughter could hand them to customers, Dalton saw Mr. Wong peek out. Mrs. Wong was speaking loudly in the background. Maybe Wong's diner had become trendy in the last couple years, with university kids driving down from USC and some of the young movie star kids cruising in from Malibu for late-night beers, but the clientele in the diner now were used to the street. The guy with dirty hair took one look at Dalton, his jacket draped over one arm, and dropped his eating utensils and headed for the door. The fat man with pink legs ran out while still chewing. Mr. Wong came through the kitchen door and grabbed his daughter by the shoulder. He pulled her away from the register and disappeared into the kitchen.

"Jason Dalton. That's the name you go by now, isn't it?" The woman looked at him with a little smirk.

Dalton jumped on top of her and grabbed the microphone from her ear and ripped the cord off. He shoved her across the booth and sat down beside her. "I don't give a damn about names. Who the hell are you working for?"

Her first punch cut Dalton's cheek and snapped his head back.

He blocked the second punch and shoved the muzzle of his 9-mm into her nose, and spit blood on her blouse. "You hit like a girl."

Two loud shots rattled the windows.

The woman jumped.

Without moving his eyes from the woman's face, Dalton called, "Nick, are you hit?"

CHAPTER 9

"I'm okay," laughed Nick. "My .45 gets two thumbs up on Facebook. I blasted a hole right through the side of the trailer. Some sneaky little guy pointed a machine gun at me."

"Is he still out there?"

"His body is."

The woman took a deep breath and swallowed; she folded her hands on the table. "I think we got off on the wrong foot. I represent the Israeli government. I've been sent to retrieve an artifact that was stolen from my country."

"That's a good story. Governments go through diplomatic channels, though." Dalton patted her down, ran his hand over her arms and around her waist.

She jerked when he reached between her legs.

"I watched a friend get sliced up because he was too shy to check for weapons between a woman's legs," he said.

She cursed in Hebrew and closed her eyes. "There, are you satisfied?"

"I don't take chances with my life."

"Are you going to put the gun away?" she said.

"No. If you move, I'm going to ruin your silk blouse."

"You have such a way with words. Mr. Dalton, we know you were hired to find Solomon's Key. It belongs to the people of Israel. I am going to take it into custody and return it to its rightful owner."

"And that rightful owner, would that be a private party, a rich person, maybe a general?"

"My employer wants to remain anonymous. Now I'm going to signal my associates, and they're going to take away our dead friend." The woman raised her arm and made a circle in the air, as though twirling a lasso.

Out in the parking lot, a door opened and two men wearing military fatigues, jumped from an SUV. They trotted over and disappeared behind the diner. After a moment they came back into view dragging the dead man.

"I'm sure the police have been alerted. They're probably en route. You've got one driveway to exit. I think you're going to get a surprise on your way out," said Dalton.

The woman smiled with amusement in her eyes. "The police can't search a diplomat's vehicle."

"You're not a diplomat. You're a hired thug with diplomatic immunity. Big difference. If I find you in my client's house or on her property, I'll kill you." Dalton shoved his weapon into its holster.

"There are six words in Hebrew that describe you perfectly." The woman slid across the booth, pushed off the table, and stood up, then hurried through the restaurant.

As the SUVs turned on their lights and rolled across the parking lot, Nick came out of the shadows and sat down.

Dalton watched the taillights disappear. "I got a feeling we need to watch Sophie Devonshire's house tonight," he said.

"Are you talking about hiding in bushes, with bugs and reptiles and mice sneaking around where you can't even see them?"

"Pretty much. I don't think Mrs. Devonshire knows what she's gotten into."

"Or maybe she knows, and she's playing us." Nick lifted the .45 and sniffed the muzzle.

"Man, Nick, what happened?"

"What do you mean?"

Dalton laughed. "Your forehead is bleeding."

"The gun kicked so hard it hit me in the head. Don't laugh. It hurts."

* * *

After they left the diner, Nick searched with his phone, made some calls and found that Sophie Devonshire was staying in her Long Beach residence, tucked away on Naples Island, in the middle of Alamitos Bay.

By the time they drove to Naples, the sun was setting. Behind the high-rises of downtown, the last rays of sunlight turned thin wisps of cloud orange and red.

Sophie Devonshire's long box house sat squeezed between houses on three sides. A sidewalk separated the tiny front yard from a canal.

Dalton walked down the sidewalk. "I have to park a block away," he told Nick. "The neighbors are close enough to touch. How am I supposed to watch her house without being seen?"

Nick stared at a boat gliding along the canal. "Maybe we should get one of those."

Dalton followed his gesture. "Schnauzer Rentals," he read.

Nick did a quick search and found the rental agency was located across the bay. They drove over and rented one of the boats for the night. By the time they got back to the canal, colored lights were shining around the *Queen Mary* and the oil islands. And out past the silhouette of downtown, the Vincent Thomas Bridge was a ribbon of brake lights that faded into the night.

Across from Sophie Devonshire's house, they pulled up to a small dock and tied the bow line. They removed cushions from the seats, placed them on the floor, and sat down so they might not be seen. Then they waited.

After half an hour, Nick whispered: "We're going to find that artifact, right boss?"

"That woman at the diner called it Solomon's Key."

"Maybe that's why I couldn't get information about it. I didn't have the name."

"If her husband had it, we'll find it."

"Was it bad that I shot that guy?"

Dalton looked at Nick. "First time?"

"Yeah."

A cold marine layer had rolled in off the Pacific. Out at the end of the jetty, where the bay opened to the ocean, a white fog moved toward them.

"Don't feel bad. If you didn't shoot him he might have shot you. One of the customers could have been killed. Maybe you contained the situation. He wasn't carrying a combat rifle for nothing."

"Yeah." Nick buttoned his coat and flipped up the collar. "Why don't you and that Jax woman just get away? If I had a woman special like you say…."

"She's moved on, buddy."

Three hours passed. Nick fell asleep after a long battle of trying to hold his head up.

Dalton shoved his hands into his pockets and waited. As the hours rolled past, some people hurried to their homes. A couple passed carrying groceries in brown paper bags. A man passed with a heavy briefcase over his shoulder. Around midnight, a man and woman, yawning, their hair messy from bed, pushed a stroller along the sidewalk. The baby in the stroller cried.

Then, a few hours before sunrise Dalton watched a stocky dark figure walk up the sidewalk and stop. He wanted to turn on his phone and check the time, but Nick had eliminated that option.

Dalton shook his head, focused his eyes and snapped awake. There was something familiar about the way the guy moved: decisive, like a hunting dog with the scent of bird in its nostrils. It was the bald killer from the office.

Dalton slowly got to his knees, leaned over, and put a hand over Nick's mouth and shook him.

Nick's eyes popped open. Dalton put a finger across his lips

39

and pointed to the house. He took his hand away and whispered, "Our bald friend just showed up."

Nick leaned forward and touched the .45 clipped to his belt. "The guy from the office? Tell me I can shoot him. Where can I shoot him? In the leg, can I shoot him in the leg?"

"No," said Dalton. "This guy's mine. We need to find out where the money is coming from. That'll tell us a lot. Number one rule of detective work: follow the money."

There was dew on the hand-rails as they climbed the gangplank to the sidewalk. Dalton walked on tip-toes to Sophie Devonshire's house. He looked about and grabbed Nick.

"Where'd he go?" He hurried to the gate, reached and opened it and crept along between the houses, his feet crunching on the gravel walkway. He hadn't gone more than half the length of the house when a light came on upstairs. His instinct told him to get off the walkway, so he pushed among the bushes that lined the fence. There he squatted, with leaves touching his face, and something shoved against his ribs. After ten minutes, the light turned off, so he came out of the hiding place and walked on the grass to the tiny back yard, where he peeked around the corner of the house.

A dark figure moved about a window. The intruder had a suction-cup device pressed against the window. It made the sound of cutting glass.

Dalton got close enough to strike before the guy raised up.

The second before the first blow hit him in the back of the head, the intruder turned. Dalton's punch brushed his scalp.

The burglar's left hand came down on Dalton's shoulder. At the same time, he tried to knee Dalton in the groin.

Dalton jerked his leg up and blocked the knee, then shot both hands forward and tried to disable the guy with a thumb to his eye, but missed.

The assailant head butted him in the cheek, and Dalton groaned and recovered quickly and connected with an upper cut that caught the guy on the chin and sent him staggering back. As the guy stumbled, Dalton hit him twice in the head.

The man dropped to his knees and aimed a pistol.

Dalton too had drawn his weapon. "Where's the money coming from? Why is that artifact so important?" he said in a low, angry voice.

The man smiled and shook his head. "You don't even know the story, do you?"

Somewhere out over the city, he heard a helicopter. A moment later a bright spotlight swept over houses and trees and the backyard lit up like a bright summer day.

A loudspeaker in the sky said: "This is the Long Beach Police Department. Lower your weapons."

"I think we will be seeing each other again, Mr. Dalton," said the intruder. He ran to the fence and climbed over as the spotlight shifted about the backyard, as though the operator in the helicopter was trying to decide which man to follow.

Seconds later, he heard policemen shouting. And that was when he decided to place his weapon on the ground and raise his hands.

"Police! Hands behind your neck. Get on your knees."

CHAPTER 10

Dalton sat in the ambulance in front of the house while an EMT treated the gash over his eye and dabbed his swollen lip with antiseptic.

"Well, I see you met Uri." Harvey Lowenthal paced back and forth at the ambulance doors and held his jacket open while searching his vest pockets. "I told you to listen, but I'm just some stupid FBI agent. What do I know?"

Dalton looked past the agent to Sophie Devonshire. She stood on the corner surrounded by uniforms that asked questions and wrote down her responses. Even in the middle of the night, she looked good, wrapped in a silk robe, shiny black slippers on her feet. Her red hair hung in a ponytail over her shoulder and moved when she turned her head.

Floodlights lit up several houses and the sidewalk. Two boats floated in the canal, their engines shifting from forward to reverse so they could stay in one spot and watch the show. Policemen walked about. Neighbors stood clustered together among squad cars. Every few minutes one pointed at Sophie Devonshire.

"It looks like you're real popular, Dalton." Lowenthal flipped a thumb over his shoulder, gesturing to a couple of SUVs, a group of men huddled around an open door.

"That's the Israeli government woman I spoke to earlier."

"Israeli government, my ass." Agent Lowenthal signaled his

assistant with a raised finger.

The slim woman with short black hair, wearing a business suit, walked up and asked what she could help with."

"You want to show him what we got on Lizzie over there?"

The woman agent lifted the tablet she was carrying, and typed and swiped a few times and held the screen in front of Dalton. "Liza Cohen has been arrested four times for trafficking in stolen artifacts. She works for Shelomo Ben Haim, a Tel Aviv mobster and arms dealer. His dirty little fingers are in quite a few pies."

"She has a good jab."

"I thought you were supposed to be some hand-to-hand whiz kid or something." Lowenthal did his best imitation of Bruce Lee. His assistant blushed.

"Am I supposed to crack a woman?"

"In her case, yes. Half the things I've tracked in my career are probably hanging in her boss's private collection. I'd give a year of paychecks to see her put away." Lowenthal grumbled a thank-you to his assistant, and gently pushed her aside. "Look, Dalton, I'm hanging my career on getting that artifact. I'm so close I can smell it."

After the EMTs had poked and prodded, wiped Dalton's face and stuck sutures on his eyebrow, and after several police officers had asked him questions and written down his answers, checked his license to carry a concealed weapon and the numbers on his gun, he was free to go.

He wanted to get away from this scene, the lights and neighbors. He started to rush down the sidewalk. But then he saw Sophie Devonshire. She looked weak and afraid, and he wanted to help her. So instead of walking away and getting in his car and getting back on the road, back on the bridge into the city, he went over and put his arm around her.

"Mrs. Devonshire, I'm sorry–"

"It is Sophie, remember?"

"Sophie—I'm sorry to ask more questions, but if we want to get past this, we have to know all the details of your husband's life. Is there a house or an apartment that he frequented?" He walked beside her to the open front door.

Sophie Devonshire pushed him away and stepped back. "Mr. Dalton, I'm not sure I like what you're implying. My husband and I were close. He didn't have another woman. I would've known. Is that what you are trying to ask?" She closed her eyes.

"There are hard questions I have to ask. I ask, and we move along. That's how it works. You hired me to find that artifact and to find out if your husband had another life. If I'm going to do that, I need to look through his things."

Before she could respond, a police officer walked over and asked for her signature. Men and women cops crossed the lawn and one by one they climbed in their cars and drove off. The ambulance too pulled away, and since the helicopter had long since disappeared, there was nothing more for the neighbors to look at, and they went home.

When they were finally alone, Sophie walked into the house. Dalton closed the door and flipped the lock.

"I believe you asked about my husband."

"Yes," said Dalton. "Did he have any storage containers? Warehouses? A property that needed his work quite a bit? A favorite get-away?"

"My, you are persistent." Sophie Devonshire hurried around the room. Even though the drapes were pulled and the blinds closed, she walked from one window to another, checking them, tugging the drapes to fully cover the windows. "I just hate the neighbors watching. I thought I'd have some privacy here on the island."

After she checked the windows, she stopped in the center of the dining room and touched the table. "Yes, Mr. Dalton, my husband spent a lot of time out of the country, but after he passed, I was searching through his papers and discovered there were several days here and there over the years when I thought he was abroad or in another state, when he was actually in the small house we keep up in San Pedro. I guess it was his home away from home. We didn't go there more than a few times, so I was quite surprised to find receipts from various services around San Pedro: a plumber, electrician, lawn mowing, an architect."

"I need to get in there. Do you have the keys or passwords?"

She sat on the sofa and cried into her hands. "I don't know. I wish I'd never seen that artifact."

From atop a steamer trunk wet bar, Dalton opened a bottle of twenty-five-year-old scotch, and poured two fingers into a glass, walked over and touched Mrs. Devonshire on the shoulder. "I know it's early morning, but I think you need this."

"Thank you." She drank half and turned the glass in her hand. "It's not that someone I loved is gone. What hurts is the empty places left in my life that were once filled."

Dalton set beside her. His shoulder touched hers. "That's the hardest thing. You have to learn to fill those voids. You can't stop and think about the other person. You find something to do when you feel the pain coming, and you don't ask any questions. You just go and do it."

"Sometimes I feel so weak, like I don't want to try." She leaned against him and cried again.

"It's okay. I got you. Just let it out." Jason Dalton wrapped his arm around her.

* * *

He met Nick in the Starbucks in Belmont Shore, a trendy suburb where the beautiful people, carrying tiny dogs in bags, strolled the shopping street wearing the latest fashions. It was the only place he could think of that was busy so early, and having people around meant safety. He hurried past the line of shiny choppers parked in front of Starbucks, wondering for a second how the owners earned a living, pushed open the front door, and took his place in line. With his drink in hand, he moved to a high metal table against the wall.

Nick raised his chin from a laptop. "This is a hell of a case, right boss?"

"It's a storm, that's for sure. Those particle samples you sent out—did you get word back?" Dalton sipped his coffee.

"First things first," said Nick, and pushed a white plastic bag across the table.

"What's that?"

"It's a burner phone. We're going to buy a new one every other day. New rules. Don't look at me that way. You pay me for my computer skills. The guys tracking you are high tech, so we adapt, right?"

Dalton pulled a box from the bag and opened it.

"Okay," said Nick. "Now, back to that sample I sent out: the guy texted me thirty minutes ago. It sounded like he was jumping up and down, he was so excited. We're heading over there."

"You can tell that from a text?"

"It's a millennial thing. Don't try it. You might get hurt." Nick tapped his phone and raised it above his head. "I just need directions. I hate this cheapo carrier." He smiled and looked around the café, then asked Google for directions.

Dalton removed the plastic lid from his coffee and sipped. "I don't have to ride in your flower-power bug, do I?"

Nick stood up. "No. You can call Uber if you get your phone working."

* * *

Google spoke every time they turned or approached a traffic light. The guy lived in Signal Hill, a small city surrounded by Long Beach. For decades it had been a no-man's land of cliffs, creaking oil wells, tumbleweeds rolling down the street, and coyotes. During the eighties the ugly fields began to change. Developers and oil companies capped the wells and hauled in clean soil and built trendy, gated communities, filled with cookie-cutter shiny houses.

As they drove up the hill, Nick picked up his phone and read, "I am near Shell Hill with a running group."

In the distance a group of men and women, a few wearing jogging suits, others dressed in T-shirts and gym trunks, stretched their legs on the guard rail and did calisthenics. A mile behind them, a jetliner was gliding down onto a runway.

Nick pulled to the curb and they got out and walked toward the runners. An Indian man in his thirties, his hair messed up and twenty pounds of extra weight around his gut, trotted over, shaking his hands in the air.

"Are you Nick?" he asked with an Indian accent.

Nick held up his cell phone, revealing the man's text message, and said he was.

"I work at the university lab and analyzed those samples you brought for me. This is incredible because they date to five-hundred years BC." He shook his arms about and wobbled his head.

"Whoa, buddy, take it easy." Dalton grabbed his arm. "It's okay. Just tell us what you found."

The guy put his hand on his chest and breathed heavily, as though he'd just run a sprint. "Okay, okay, like I said, I analyzed the sample in the vial you gave me, but the most fascinating part is the history of the object in the photo. In all my life I never dreamed that I, Singh, would come across such a fabulous piece of history. And I have it all written down for your benefit. If you would like to come to my apartment, I would be happy to show you what I found. It is a relic that people have been fighting over for centuries, and it is here in the city. It is so exciting."

"Why are you so excited?" asked Dalton.

"Can you not see? Did you not hear the words I just spoke?"

"I heard, but–"

Nick turned a circle and said, "Oh man, boss, I'm sorry. I thought this guy was legit."

"Legit," shouted the Indian man, slapping one hand onto the palm of the other. "I have a PhD in Philology, and can prove to you that that artifact is a map."

Dalton pulled Nick away and whispered: "The guy is crazy.

47

Let's get out of here."

"Crazy?" shouted the Indian man. "No, sir, I am a respectable scholar. Look me up on your Google. Go on. That is a map to one of the world's most fabulous treasures. You got me involved in this, now you have to protect me or send me back to India. I saw people sitting in a car outside my apartment this morning. How do they know about the map? All I did was ask a few colleagues about it online. You must hide me. I need protection." He kept pulling his T-shirt from the folds of his belly.

"Okay, Mr. Singh. Take it easy." Dalton patted his shoulder. "Nothing's going to happen to you, okay? Why don't you take us to your place and show us what you found?"

Mr. Singh waved to his running group. Two of the women shouted goodbye and said they'd see him next time.

※ ※ ※

He lived above an old industrial building with concrete walls and a rollup garage door that faced the street. Once they parked, Mr. Singh led them up a rusting staircase, fumbled with his keys, found the correct one, and pushed open the door. Once they crossed the threshold, he closed the door and shoved a two-by-four under the doorknob and wedged it against the floor.

"Serious lock," said Dalton.

Mr. Singh rushed across the apartment to a Persian rug. Atop the rug stood two sawhorses that held a plywood desk. A laptop sat in front of a padded chair at one end. Around the chair lay computer circuits and an old monitor.

The one-room apartment smelled of curry and was large enough to fit eight cars. A row of metal lockers, covered with old decals, lined the wall in the kitchen area. Facing those stood an old knee-high soda pop refrigerator.

"It's right here." He pulled a thick encyclopedia from a shelf and opened it at a paper marker. "After I carbon dated it, I did some research. There's only a few references to it through history, and it's difficult to separate myth from fact. But that photograph looks very similar to what was called Solomon's Key. And Solomon's Key was supposed to be a map to Solomon's mines."

"Solomon?" Nick hunched his shoulders.

"Yes, Solomon, son of King David. Are you with me? Oh, my God, I am working with imbeciles. King Solomon, the Old Testament, Jewish history? Forget it. The text looks Sumerian in that photo, and I transposed some Khitan and Sanskrit to fill in, and ran it through a computer program one of my colleagues wrote up, and anyway, I was able to decipher some coordinates."

"Do you mean a location? Are you telling me you can calculate the location of Solomon's mines?" said Dalton.

"Yes, and bad men will kill to get that information. You will buy me a ticket to India, yes? I'll disappear. I'll slip away in Kashmir and pray in the temple every day. Why did you send this horrible thing to me? They will send bad, professional killers to find it, and I am just a simple scholar."

Dalton paced back and forth beside the rug and covered his mouth.

"Please, I am sorry I called you an imbecile. I want very much to see my family in India. I only want to leave before nasty men with guns, like the ones that were watching my apartment earlier, come to find my calculations."

"Stop," demanded Dalton. "You were making guesses with languages, right? I mean you were just working from a photo."

"Yes Mr. Dalton. But that just proves what I could do with the real Solomon's Key. I could decipher it and find a location."

Dalton stopped pacing. "If that's true, then we may be in trouble."

Nick moved from the study and was fiddling with the red curtains that glowed with the sunlight trying to enter. He reached above his head and pulled them aside, and light flooded the room through the industrial windows.

The first shot made a clean entrance hole through one of the panes. The thud when it hit the glass was the only sound it made. It was such a silent attack that Nick didn't react. He stood searching the windows, wondering what had broken the pane. During that moment of reasoning, another shot hit the glass. By that time, Nick knew what was happening.

"Get down!" he shouted, and dove behind the door.

The third shot hit a statue of Krishna on the desk. The next one hit the encyclopedia in Mr. Singh's hand. The impact knocked the book against his chest.

Dalton pulled him to the wall behind the refrigerator. Mr. Singh shrieked and shouted and threw his arms about.

"Nick," said Dalton. "Can you see where the shots came from?" On his hands and knees, he fought to restrain Mr. Singh while peeking around the edge of the refrigerator. "No, Nick, don't—"

Nick already had the two-by-four lock in his hand, and was opening the door. He threw the board aside and pulled the door open as bullets burst through the door. Sunlight entered through each hole like a tiny flashlight beam. Nick shouted and ran onto the staircase and fired three shots at the rooftop of the building across the street.

They didn't wait around to find out who'd fired the shots. That person was probably long gone. But Dalton didn't take any chances, either, as he led Mr. Singh down the vibrating staircase, his weapon drawn, Nick following behind.

On the street they stopped at Nick's Volkswagen. Dr. Singh grabbed the roof of the car like a child refusing to get in. The car rocked back and forth as Dalton tried to shove the heavy man into the back seat.

"Get in, Singh, or I'll shoot you myself." Dalton pulled back the action of his automatic.

Singh's eyes got large, and he spun around and pressed his back against the roof of the Volkswagen.

"This is America, and you want me to escape in a Volkswagen bug? You should be ashamed."

Dalton ran around to the other side of the car and pushed Nick out of the way; he climbed into the backseat. "Stay here and get shot, I don't care. Nick, get us the hell out of here. Drive."

Mr. Singh climbed in with a groan. "I don't know what is worse: to be shot in America or have my family learn I escaped a shootout in a Volkswagen."

Dalton shoved his pistol into its holster and looked about the streets. Then he pushed Nick. "He's embarrassed to be seen in your car."

Nick turned. "My car drove all the way from New York. It survived flash floods and blazing Mojave heat. Bugsy gets twenty-four miles to the gallon on the highway. You can get out where you like."

Mr. Singh reached over, took the shoulder belt and wrapped it around himself, then looked out the rear windshield as he latched the buckle. "Krishna help us," he said, wagging his head about and pointing behind the car. "Mr. Nick, drive fast and don't look back."

"Oh my god," said Dalton. "You named your car Bugsy?"

"Shut your mouth." Nick turned the key. The engine cranked over but didn't start.

"You got to be kidding," shouted Dalton, waving his gun. "If I fucking shoot Bugsy, will he start?"

"He always starts." Nick turned the key and the engine cranked and cranked and finally started. But it was too late.

Dalton was thrown against the window as a black Cadillac SUV smashed the side of the bug. For a moment the Caddy stood still, then lurched forward and shoved the Volkswagen against the curb. The passenger window rolled down halfway, and a man stuck his head out and laughed.

"Oh, I'm so sorry. You have nowhere to go. Isn't that a shame?"

Another SUV screeched to a halt behind the first, and the doors flew open. Three men and a woman jumped out and walked toward the Volkswagen. Nick rocked back and forth in his seat and hit the dashboard with his fist. "Oh, so I got nowhere to go?" He reached beneath his jacket and pulled out his father's .45. He aimed it at the man in the window.

The guy jumped out of view when he saw the gun.

Nick didn't have room to stick the gun out the window and shoot, so he popped a round through his own windshield and put out the front tire of the Cadillac. "Here, you! Take this," he said, and tossed the pistol onto Mr. Singh's lap.

Mr. Singh picked it up as though he didn't know which end was which, fumbled with it, pointed it through the shattered windshield, and shot into the engine compartment of the SUV. But the .45 jumped violently, and he discharged two more rounds by accident through the roof of the Volkswagen before Dalton grabbed the weapon out of his hand.

"Oh, I got nowhere to go?" Nick shoved the gear shift into reverse and dumped the clutch, and the bug lurched backward and hit a parked motorcycle at full speed, knocking it onto the hood of parked car.

"Holy crap, Nick! An hour ago, you were a computer nerd. What happened?" Dalton discharged the clip from the .45 and counted four rounds, shoved it back into the pistol.

"I'm pissed." Nick shoved the gear shift forward and turned the wheel into the curb. But the curb was too high for the VW, and he shifted into reverse, rolled back a foot, then hit first gear and stomped on the gas. One of the rear wheels spun and smoked, then got traction, and the bug shot forward and jumped the curb.

The car bounced and threw Dalton off the backseat and into the air, where he hit his head against the ceiling.

The Volkswagen crossed the sidewalk and crashed against a stucco retaining wall. But it didn't stop. It bounced off and screeched along, hugging the wall as the motor raced. Nick fought with the steering wheel and raced up the sidewalk until he got wedged between a parked car and the retaining wall. But he wouldn't give up.

Dalton pushed between the seats and raised his legs and kicked the rear window. "Get us out of here!"

Nick shoved it into reverse and revved the engine and popped the clutch, and the car hopped up and lurched and spun a tire, then pulled free and raced down the sidewalk backward, bouncing off the retaining wall and crashing into three parked cars before it dropped over the curb behind the SUV, did a quick little turn, and took off down the road.

Dalton kicked, and the rear window fell out. He jumped up and fired two rounds into the SUV. "They're coming, Nick!" he shouted.

They flew into the first turn so fast that the car turned sideways and Dalton thought it was going to flip over as it climbed up onto the two right wheels. It probably would've fell over on its side, but an SUV slammed into it and pushed it along the street sideways, the tires hopping across the asphalt. Suddenly the Volkswagen hit a patch of rough asphalt, and the tires found traction and the Volkswagen shot free.

Nick was revving the engine so high that when it finally did gain traction, the car took off backward so quickly that he couldn't react fast enough. Bugsy raced up an asphalt driveway, crashed through a twenty-foot-high wall of shrubs, and flew off an embankment. The men shouted as the car left the ground.

It came down hard, hit and bounced, left the ground again, and stopped at the bottom of the steep grade carved with gullies. Twenty feet away stood an abandoned oil derrick. The dirt was stained black.

Nick hit his door with his shoulder several times. With each blow it creaked and opened a few inches, then the door dropped to the ground and fell over.

"Am I alive?" Dalton climbed to a sitting position.

Nick was the first to unfasten his seatbelt. He dropped out of the car onto his knees, shook his head, and stepped to the car and helped the others get out.

Once out of the vehicle, they gathered behind the car on their hands and knees. Dalton looked out over the top of the smashed bug to the embankment. Men were running about. One of the SUVs sped off.

"They're coming, Nick. How many rounds you have left?"

Nick pulled out the clip and counted his remaining bullets.

"Four rounds. I don't know what happened to my other clips."

"You had to send me this death project. I'm a good Hindu. I only wanted to get back to India to see my mother before she died." Mr. Singh lowered his face to the ground, as though praying.

"We're not dead yet, Singh," said Dalton. "Come on, they'll be down here in a minute. Let's get out of here."

Mr. Singh moaned and shrieked when he climbed to his feet, and collapsed in pain. "My ankle! I think I broke my ankle in that ugly little car."

Nick and Dalton each took an arm around their shoulders and carried him past the oil well and out to the road. They had just reached the black-top when the first SUV screeched to a halt.

Dalton threw the arm from around his shoulder, dropped to one knee, and aimed his weapon. But it was no use.

Three men climbed out of the SUV, each aiming a combat rifle with a laser scope. A second SUV stopped behind the first. Two men and a woman hurried over and took position.

"There is no reason to die here," said Dalton, climbing to his feet.

The woman from the diner smiled and stepped in front of her associates.

"That was some good driving," she called. "I need that program that Dr. Singh was bragging about in an email. I'm taking it whether you're alive or dead."

"Singh," shouted Nick. "You mentioned it online?"

"Maybe. I might have told a friend that I was onto a discovery."

The loud chopping sound of a helicopter stopped all talk. It appeared over the ridge, hovering above them, its loudspeaker blaring.

"This is the FBI. Put down your weapons!"

The woman and her associates looked at each other, not knowing if they should shoot the helicopter out of the sky or run to the vehicles.

They didn't have long to consider. Moments after the helicopter appeared, FBI vehicles rolled onto the street from both directions. Agents jumped out and dove to the dirt with automatic weapons and shotguns pointed at the Israelis.

The woman cussed and stomped a foot.

Harvey Lowenthal climbed out of a car and put a bullhorn to his mouth. "Put down your weapons or die on foreign soil. I will not ask again. I'm going to count to five before we cut you down."

The Israeli agents set their weapons on the road.

"Never again," said Dalton. "You never drive again."

"Bugsy saved us."

CHAPTER 11

They drove down Shell Hill in an FBI vehicle. On the edge of Signal Hill, where concrete, industrial buildings met the tract homes of Long Beach, they turned into a driveway behind a long brick building that had once been a National Guard facility.

As they waited for the electric gate to open, eight protestors surrounded the car and waved picket signs that read: WE LIVE HERE, NO GOV. SECRETS, and SPIES OUT. Men and women, their children beside them, shouted: "Spies must go!" over and over.

Soon Dalton and Nick found themselves in a lecture hall with tiered seating. Several agents walked in with briefcases. A female agent carried in a laptop and joined the others on the stage.

A few minutes later, Harvey Lowenthal walked across the hall and said with a loud voice, "Okay, agent Murkowski, why don't you open?"

An agent stood up and hoisted his belt buckle, crossed the stage, pressed the button on the wall, and a large television screen turned on. "Sir," he said, "from the beginning?"

"We discussed this yesterday, agent Murkowski. Yes, from the very beginning."

An illustration of Solomon's Key appeared on the screen. "An artifact stolen from the Vatican just after Martin Luther, recently came to our attention in Germany."

The image on the screen changed to photographs of a barroom crime scene.

"So, it surfaced in Germany and disappeared after this attack. We believe Uri Dent led the assault. He is working for the Rapid Intervention Group, which is part of the Gendarmerie Corps of Vatican City State. They are a special forces unit."

"Uri Dent, a.k.a. the Snake," shouted Harvey Lowenthal. "Does that name sound familiar, Dalton?"

"Why are you showing this to me?"

"Because," said Harvey Lowenthal. "I'm hoping some of it will sink into your thick skull. We need to find that artifact, and we need your help."

Dalton stood up. "What are you going to do with it?"

"That is out of my hands."

"I've heard that before. Isn't it funny how a treasure makes governments forget about the law?" Dalton flicked Nick on the shoulder. "Come on, we're out of here."

One of the agents stood up and walked to the door with his hand on his holstered weapon. "Boss?" said the agent when he reached exit.

"Look, thanks for the show. I appreciate it. But we're not under arrest, so we're leaving."

Harvey Lowenthal waved a hand, and his agent stepped away from the door. "Look Dalton, you're free to go. But that artifact is stolen property. It's our job to return it to its owner."

Dalton and Nick walked across the room. When they reached the exit, Dalton stopped. "And because you can't figure out who it belongs to, well, you'll just lock it up while you locate the treasure, right?"

Dalton pushed open the heavy door and squinted in the sunlight.

"You need to come back in here," said Lowenthal. "I have something for you."

Dalton looked into the room. Once his eyes adjusted, he saw on the screen what looked like an old image of himself in military uniform. "Really? You had to dig that up? I'm never amazed how low you feds are willing to go. What? Now you're going to blackmail me? Man, you guys just wallow in shit. How do you keep your shirts white?"

"I got the results back on your fingerprints. It's a new day and age when the Federal Bureau of Investigation is actually sharing information with the Department of Defense and the Justice Department. Glory be." Lowenthal waved his hands.

The image changed, and the agent continued. "Here we have young Mr. Dalton in army uniform in 2005."

"Do you know how many lives you just put at risk?" asked Dalton.

"But you dropped out of sight in 2014. A source tells me you were given a new identity in exchange for testimony against the cartels."

Harvey Lowenthal slapped a file on the table beside Dalton.

Before the agent withdrew his hand, Dalton spun Lowenthal's arm behind his back. He snatched the agent's weapon and shoved it under Lowenthal's chin.

"How does it feel to have your life put at risk?" Dalton backed away as agents moved toward him. With one hand he ejected the clip from Lowenthal's weapon, kicked it across the floor, and tossed the weapon onto a table. The pistol slid across the surface and dropped to the floor. "Tell your men to back away, or I'll snap your arm at the shoulder." He shook Lowenthal and repeated the threat.

"That's assault on a federal agent."

"You threaten to expose my identity. That would put my life and the life of all my loved ones in danger: men, women, and children. But when I threaten back, wow, you get all worked up and say I assaulted a federal agent. You make me sick. Nick, take photos of them and the images they showed us. Take the files too. I think the *Times* will be interested. I'm sure my attorney will be peachy happy to see all this."

"Back up," said Lowenthal. "Everyone, stay calm. Put your weapons away."

Dalton put his lips to the agent's ear and whispered: "Remember what you read in my file about sniper training, Lowenthal? If you make my information public, and one of my family is hurt, you won't even hear the shot. Understand?"

"Yes."

"I guess we can't drive your bug," Dalton told Nick, still holding the agent.

Nick finished snapping photos. "Not hardly. But Uber is on the way."

They ran across the parking lot and climbed into a Prius with the Uber symbol on the windshield.

"Are they going to come after us?" Nick said, turning to look back.

"A little station like that, I don't think so."

CHAPTER 12

Dalton leaned forward and told the driver, "Drive down by the beach and head north along Ocean. Take us downtown and just keep driving around until we tell you different." After the driver agreed, Dalton looked at Nick.

"You knew all that stuff Lowenthal was going on about anyways, right?"

Nick grabbed onto the safety strap hanging at the top of the window, put his hand through it, and lifted up on the seat and repositioned himself. "Well, yeah, most of it. I had to know who I was working for."

"I need to go somewhere tonight. But I need to know that Sophie Devonshire is safe. Can you stay with her?"

"Of course. You're going to see that Jax woman, right?"

Dalton turned. "Yeah, if my past is exposed she's in danger. I need to make sure she's safe too."

"If she's so terrific like you said, why don't you just forget about all this and run away with her?"

"For one, Sophie Devonshire's life is in danger. And besides, I don't know if Jax still wants me."

"There's one way to find out."

"This isn't the best time to bring a woman onboard. There's so much going on, it makes me crazy."

"Makes *you* crazy? Ha! I'm a computer guy, and I find out my boss is being chased by a military hit squad. He's been relocated by the DOD, and the fricking Israeli government is trying to shoot him. I'm carrying a cannon around like a gangster rapper. Hell, any person on the street might jump me and slit my throat. And talking about some girl makes you nervous?"

"You ever met a woman that just looked in your eyes and knew everything about you?"

"You're still in love with her. Go and get her and make a life."

Dalton looked up at the Uber driver. "Watch the road, driver. Keep your ears closed and drive."

The driver leaned toward the steering wheel, reached up and jerked on his shoulder harness, and said: "Yes, sir. Yes, I can do that. I am not listening to one word you say, not about the hit squad or the people that want to slit your throat. Nothing. Me, Abdul, he hears nothing because you tip him very well."

Dalton tapped Nick on the leg. "I'm bringing in someone to help."

"Okay." Nick shoved his hair back.

"Wait a minute. You already know about my buddy from the military. You found the e-mails where I asked him for information about Jax. That's why you have that dog-ate-the-cookies look on your face."

"Yes, yes, yes." Nick thumped the head-rest of the seat in front of him. "Computers. Everything you do on a computer is recorded. I'm a computer guy. I can't not look at that stuff. When I came to work for you I didn't know who you were. I had to find out, all right?"

"So why do you let me explain everything, if you already know? I hate computers."

"Good. Of course you do. Cross the bridge to LA. See your buddy and get an update on Jax." Nick rolled down the window and his hair flew about.

✽ ✽ ✽

Rain had fallen earlier in the day for all of five minutes, and the radio weather was filled with storm reports. Dalton smiled because whenever it rained in LA, it was a storm, and people spoke about it as though some illegal action had taken place.

He accelerated up onto the Vincent Thomas Bridge. In the distance, Palos Verdes Peninsula stuck out into the Pacific, dark and rough and specked with lights. Halfway over the bridge, he had to slow down as wisps of fog came in off the ocean and drifted across the bridge. This route made him feel good, as though he was out of the city.

Dalton pulled off the bridge, drove along some residential streets to the 110 Freeway, and headed straight into downtown LA. The off-ramp dropped him into the warehouses of the arts district. This had once been a hustling industrial section where semis pulled up to loading docks, their trailers filled with textiles, paper products, coffee, and food. Now the neighborhood was filled with chic art galleries, clothing boutiques that played loud music, artist lofts, cafés and street musicians.

The wide streets that once accommodated hundreds of trucks now seemed nearly empty, even during rush hour. Street murals added bright color to some buildings. Loud music blared from a few warehouse stores. Manikins posed on the sidewalks before clothing boutiques. Geraniums filled window pots.

Dalton searched for a corner warehouse he remembered. He smiled when he found it. A few blocks away, he waited for a car to pull out of its spot, then backed in and turned off the engine.

Outside the door, he thumped a brass tapper against the door and pressed his thumb over the spy hole. There were some noises inside the building, followed by silence.

"You got no business here, homie," someone shouted from behind the door. "I got a .357 pushed against this door that's gunna blow a hole right through it. You best move along."

Dalton chuckled. "I believe this is the rainy season in Honduras."

"Fuck me. Dalton? Is that you?"

Dalton heard keys rattling, and the four deadbolts started clicking this way and that, and after a minute the door opened, and Ted pulled him inside.

"Oh, man, it's good to see you. I'll never forget that mission in Honduras. We were bad men."

They hugged, and Dalton backed away quickly, holding his friend at arm's length. "Ted, I'm coming in hot. I got trouble coming at me from all directions. I'll understand if you don't want any part of this. Just say so, and I'll disappear."

Ted pushed him aside, picked up his door-side shotgun, and looked through the spy hole. "Who's after you? Police? Let the fuckers come. They better have a tank, because that's the only way they're getting into my crib."

"I don't think I was followed. Can you help with this case?"

Ted walked across the warehouse to an area where the concrete floor was covered with wood planks. A picnic table stood in the center. He sat the shotgun on the table and took a couple bottles of beer from an old fridge.

"Thanks." Dalton drank.

"So, we're not going to check on Jax like usual? She's doing really well with that district attorney job. Investigator. She's following your lead."

"I'm glad she's safe. I owe you for looking after her. But I can't check on her tonight."

Dalton dropped a file on the table. "You better look at this."

Ted flipped through the papers. He got to a photograph of Solomon's Key and stared at it.

"That's the whole case right there. Mrs. Devonshire's husband had it slipped into his belongings in Germany. Someone with major money is tracking it."

"How much green we talking?" Ted drank.

"Hey, you need to know what you're getting into. These guys are killers."

"Oh hell, Dalton, I grew up in Compton. I been dealing with gang bangers my whole life."

"Oh, and there's—"

"There's more?" Ted shouted and climbed to his feet. "Who else is looking for you?"

"Israelis."

"Is who?" Ted picked up the shotgun and looked around. "Brother, you are coming in hot. You make me nervous just talking to you."

"I want you to know what you're getting into if you're signing on."

Ted sat down, tapped the photo, and looked up. "How long we been tight?"

Dalton smiled and nodded. "We have to do this again? Why do we have to go through this every time?"

"Come on, brother, tell me now."

"I don't want to tell you again. What's wrong with you? You were there too. How come I have to tell the story every time?"

"How long we been homies?"

Dalton threw his head back and sighed. "Okay! Ever since that day in seventh grade."

"That kid was two years older and must have had thirty pounds on you. But that didn't stop you, no sir. Before that, I was always knocking your ass around on the football field. You were the smallest linebacker I ever saw, and I was having fun knocking your white ass all over the field. But every time I'd knock you down, you get back up and come at me again. Hell, I didn't even know we were friends, until that big bully called me a nigger, and you hit him in the mouth so hard he was spitting blood for a week. And then his whole crew jumped on you like they was ghetto pits tearing you apart. Ha!"

Ted slapped the table and laughed. "I think we fought his whole crew that day. I didn't even know you busted a knuckle on that guy's head until you showed up at the next football practice with a cast on your hand."

Dalton held up his right hand and made a fist. "That fracture almost kept me out of the Army."

"Man, I had to guard you all the way home every day for a

month."

"I know we're good, Ted, but don't take this case lightly."

"How much green we talking?"

"You still have a license?"

"My PI license is my bread and butter. And I'm getting really tired of doing divorce cases. It's enough to make you think that no woman in the world was ever faithful."

"I'll give you five large now, and five more if we find that thing. You good with that?"

Ted held his arms out to each side and danced.

"Oh, no, not the Ted dance."

"Oh, yeah, brother. Ten grand for big Ted. I'm feeling it."

"Remember how you used to drive the coach crazy when you'd Ted dance at football practice?" Dalton laughed.

"I'll bet you're dying to ask about Jax. I know you're thinking about it, Dalton. I know you want to tickle that up." Ted's whole face lit up as he smiled.

"How is she?"

"Well, she graduated and started working for the county as a social worker. But she couldn't keep her mouth shut and ended up hitting some guy when he put his hand on her leg. He got two stitches in his lip. You two have the same temper."

Dalton laughed. "I miss her."

"I know you do. She's a hell of a woman."

"Maybe we could just go over there so I can see her. Is she still writing those letters and stuff?"

Ted tapped the knuckle on the table and looked over a shoulder, and then turned and looked over the other. "Man, you hear that window rattling back there? I got a replacement from the Home Depot. It was marked down like forty percent off. All I have to do is get my tools—"

"Why are you changing the subject?"

Ted set his hands on the table and looked at his guest. "Because you're both out of your mind. All that cartel business is behind you. They forgot you. But you gotta go on refusing to be with this woman that you love. It's tearing you both apart."

"Is she still writing those letters?"

"Yes, to Congressmen and your commanding officer. She won't accept that you're gone."

"You think cartel men ever forget?"

Ted sat silent for a short while. "Maybe you should leave her alone. She was in therapy for two years, Dalton."

"I'm trying to do the right thing. Can you take me to see her?"

※ ※ ※

They went out to the van and Ted drove. After a short drive he pulled the van to the curb in a neighborhood that bordered East LA. Two-bedroom tract homes lined the streets. The gangs made this section of the city a no-man's-land in the eighties, but an influx of Latinos created the need for inexpensive housing. New families moved in and gave the area new life. Many of the homes were now painted bright colors: turquoise, and shades of pink. Gone were the bars that had once decorated windows and doors. Neighbors sat on porches and played with children.

"What happened to her old place?"

"I helped her move into this place about six months ago. She said she was working on some new projects with the DA, and needed more room. She got a really good deal here."

"Which place?"

Ted pointed to a long, rectangular building a few houses up the street. It looked like it had once been a store, with high concrete walls that had no windows.

Just as they were getting ready to climb out of the van, a man walked out the front door of Jax's building. He was an older man with gray hair. He walked twenty feet and paused, set a black brief case between his feet, placed a gray stingy brim hat on his head, and pulled a coat over his gray suit. A black town car pulled away from the curb and met him in the center of the street. A huge Samoan driver climbed out and walked around the back of the vehicle and opened the door.

"I got the license." Dalton scribbled on a piece of paper.

"That guy gives me the creeps."

"He's ex-military. I can smell it. You think Jax is working with him?"

"Maybe they're seeing each other. You know, some people still do that."

Dalton pulled his seatbelt across him and latched it, wiped his hands up and down on his pants. "Well, maybe she has moved on. I guess every step away from me is one in the right direction. But that's not what my gut tells me."

Ted reached out and took hold of Dalton's arm. "Brother, either you have to find a new city and just let her go, or jump back in that boat and be in a thousand percent."

Dalton started to speak, but Ted interrupted. "In or out, do you understand what I'm saying?"

"Yes, sir, I got it loud and clear."

CHAPTER 13

The next morning Dalton was at the office two hours before Nick. He started pulling chairs from other rooms, shoving plastic tables against the wall, and pulled his desk into a corner. He was sweeping dust from the mosaic floor tiles when Nick showed up with a Starbuck's tray.

"What's going on, boss?" Nick pushed open the door and stepped into the office.

Dalton smelled the coffee and his stomach growled. "I'm making room. We have a new person coming in. You can set your computer on this table." Dalton tapped the plastic table and pulled a coffee from the tray.

"This is still the Devonshire case, right?" Nick tore open a sugar packet.

"Yeah, Ted's coming down to do some footwork. I want you to set up as fast as possible, and get going on that stack of paperwork." He pointed to several files.

"What is it?"

"Tax records. All the properties, trips, expenses, everything a computer whiz like you needs to find a missing piece. Mr. Devonshire stirred up some bad people. To do that he had to be playing in some dark places. Find out."

Nick sipped his coffee, removed the stir stick and dropped it onto the carrier. "Oh, by the looks of all this paperwork, this is going to take a while. You mind if I farm this out?"

"To who?"

"Guys from the university, members of my computer group."

"This is sensitive client–"

"We could have it finished by tomorrow morning."

"Are you serious? Do it. Oh, I need you to run down this license plate."

"Okay, but that means I have–"

"It means you have to pay the help. Take the cash from the account."

Loud pounding came from the glass door, and Ted banged through the doorway carrying a rolled-up rug. He walked halfway across the office and looked the place over. "Yeah, this place isn't much, about what I expected in this neighborhood." He set the rug on a table and put his hands on his hips.

"You bring a rug every time you work a case?" Nick poked the rug and raised a corner, then sniffed his hand.

"That's not a rug. That's the carrying case for my ladies." Ted introduced himself.

"What'd you bring?" Dalton asked.

"Just a few girls to keep me company." He unrolled the rug. Inside were several rifles, a street sweeper shotgun with a huge magazine attachment, a couple revolvers, and a derringer.

Nick laughed and pointed with his coffee cup. "Looks like you're preparing for war."

The chair creaked as Dalton sat down. "Ted, Sophie Devonshire was attacked coming down the steps of her bank. The guy went after her purse." He walked to the white board and tapped it with a marker. "That's the bank address. I need you to get out there and work your magic, convince the person in charge that you need to take a look at the surveillance tape. I think it was a stakeout. I want to know who was involved and how we can get at them. Can you do that?"

Ted lifted the derby hat from his head and pointed to the board. "Of course, I can do that. I know the guard in that bank."

"Hey guys, we got company," called Nick. He rushed from the window, dropped his coffee cup, and picked up his .45. "I got five men coming up the stairs fast!" He pulled back the action on the pistol and ran to the door."

"Are they armed?" asked Dalton.

"I didn't see any weapons."

"If they're unarmed, then everybody needs to calm down."

There was movement outside the front door. The opaque glass of the door distorted the figures on the landing. Then came a knock.

"This is Commander Rossi with the Vatican's Rapid Response Unit. I am unarmed."

Dalton pulled on his shoulder holster and sat down, then waved for Nick to let the guy in.

"I'm Jason Dalton."

"I am pleased to meet you." The commander walked to the chair in front of the desk, and nodded.

Dalton stood up and shook his hand. "What can I do for you, commander?"

From his polished black shoes, to the stylish cut of his overcoat, the old guy was military. All that was missing were the stripes on his arms. "I came to appeal to your sense of fairness. Maybe we can work together to return the artifact to its rightful owners."

"I work for Mrs. Devonshire."

"I am willing to offer men, intelligence reports, equipment, if we work together."

"I will be returning the item to Mrs. Devonshire. You know the FBI is tracking it too."

The commander jumped to his feet and threw his arms out. "That fat Lowenthal, is he here?"

Dalton nodded. "Yes, and that bald guy you have working for you. I don't think diplomatic immunity is going to help when Lowenthal captures him."

"So, you refuse my offer?"

"I refuse."

"You are a fool." The commander knocked over the chair. "I could have my men burst in here at any minute."

Ted lifted the streetsweeper shotgun and pointed it at the commander. "Say the word."

"I offer cooperation and a way to recover the artifact quickly, but you refuse. You are a fool."

"You might want to take up your case with the Israeli government, too. They have a team in the city. It was dug up in Israel, right?"

The commander marched toward the door and stopped. He spoke a sentence in Italian, then switched to English. "We shall deal with them. My employer will double whatever Mrs. Devonshire is paying you."

"Funny thing about me is I'm old school. A deal is a deal. I intend to honor my contract."

The commander flipped a hand through the air, slapping an imaginary person. "You Americans, so brash and foolish. The artifact, or should I say Solomon's Key, is the property of the Vatican. Anyone who gets in my way will be treated with extreme prejudice. Good day to you."

The instant the door closed, Nick ran to it and looked at his boss.

Dalton nodded and Nick slipped out the door.

"I count five getting into the car," called Ted from the window.

Nick came back into the office. "Yeah, they all left."

Dalton opened a drawer and dug around inside until he found extra clips and shoved each one inside a pouch on his shoulder holster. When he finished stuffing the extra ammo away, he looked up. "You heard what he said. Am I the only one taking extra rounds?"

"Hell, no, of course not. What's our next move?" Ted sat the shotgun between the filing cabinets.

"After that visit, I'm taking you to meet Sophie Devonshire. She's getting a new bodyguard."

"No, I got to be on the street. I'm not gunna babysit." Ted held out a hand, as though to plead his case.

"Look, you're guarding the money. If anything happens to

Mrs. Devonshire, we won't get paid. Day and night, I need you at her side, ready for the worst. You understand? These are bad boys we're dealing with."

"Oh, I can watch money real good. But I gotta take my ladies with me, wrapped up warm in their rug."

Dalton walked to the clothing rack and picked up his blazer. "I'll visit the bank and the attorney's office. If I can identify the guy that demanded payment, then we're on a trail."

Nick lifted the stack of files and dropped it on the table. They hit with a loud thud. "And I have to search through papers. How exciting."

"And fast, Nick. Mrs. Devonshire said that she noticed some discrepancies. Look at the times when the professor was supposed to be out of the country. She circled the dates on the top file. If he wasn't abroad, then where was he? I need to know."

"Boss, do I have to sit and read?"

"You're the computer guy. No more shooting through walls. Settle down. Do your job."

Nick lowered his head. "I just love the sound that .45 makes."

"Man, you're scaring me."

Nick laughed and starting shoving papers into his bag. "My crew is waiting. I should have everything we need in the morning."

"Good."

"But that reminds me. Ted, what type of phone do you have?" asked Nick.

"I'm an iPhone guy." Ted set his phone on the desk.

"Cool." Nick flipped it over and smashed it four times with the butt of his pistol, as if hammering in a nail. Then he ran out of the office, and said in passing, "Tell him about the cell phone black-out."

"Someone's been bugging us," said Dalton. "You have to buy a burner phone."

Ted stood at the desk and pushed small pieces of his phone around with a finger. "I can't believe he did that. I got guns, and he still did that."

* * *

Sophie Devonshire's house stood on a street with several empty lots. The ones with houses had driveways kept private with wrought iron gates, immaculate flower beds and lawns, and Roman statues illuminated by perfect lighting. But her house sat alone. The field of brown weeds and dirt clods on either side made her house look too bright, like a Disneyland replica.

Dalton drove up the street to check things out. He looked at the cars parked here and there. None of them had people inside.

"Is that the house?" asked Ted, shifting about.

"Yeah, that one." There were lights on in the flower beds that illuminated palm trees, and lights on stakes bordered the driveway and brick walk. But the house itself was dark.

"This ain't right. If she's in there, why aren't the lights on? I need my shotgun."

"Easy," said Dalton. "Her car is there. She said she'd be in all night. Let's play this smart. We'll drive by and come back."

Ted looked over his shoulder. "You think the house is being watched?"

"I think so. Keep looking straight ahead." Dalton drove around the corner and turned onto another street. Two blocks away from the house, he parked and took out the cheap burner cell phone. He tried Mrs. Devonshire's number three times. Each time it rang and rang.

"She's not answering?" Ted opened his door.

"Nobody gets shot, okay?"

Dalton hurried to the trunk and fiddled with the key fob.

"You heard what that guy said in the office. You think they're going to be all nice and smiles?"

"All I'm saying is don't shoot unless you see a weapon."

Ted got his shotgun, and Dalton led the way around the side of the house and slipped in through a window. He held his automatic as though it was a flashlight, and pointed everywhere he looked.

Inside, a dim light shone down the stairwell. He inched along toward the light and slowly climbed the stairs. That was where he found her.

Sophie Devonshire was sitting on the sofa in the one lit-up room of the house. In her hand was a glass of bourbon. A half-empty bottle stood on the side table. She held a pillow to her chest.

Dalton pointed down the hall.

Ted nodded, raised the shotgun, and walked down the corridor, as though walking through a mine field.

"Sophie?" Dalton whispered, jerking the weapon right and left, scanning the room.

He called again. When no response came, he clicked off the safety of his weapon, and moved his finger from the guard to the trigger.

"I'm here," she said.

"Are you alone?"

She set the glass on the table and stood up. "Dalton, I'm very glad you're here. This is the one room in the house that doesn't have an exterior wall."

He hurried over and touched her arm. "Why are you hiding?"

She closed her eyes and tilted her face toward the ceiling. "Maybe you better see for yourself. Someone was watching me."

"The place is clear," said Ted.

"Where are they?" asked Dalton.

She led them to the master bedroom and was about to step through the doorway into the room when Dalton stopped her.

"Let me go first, okay?" He stepped around her and opened the bedroom door with the muzzle of his automatic. "Ted, take your safety off."

"Hell, it ain't never been on. Mrs. Devonshire," said Ted, nodding quickly, "you get behind me where I can protect you."

Dalton stepped into the room, and after a moment he said it was clear.

Ted led Sophie Devonshire into the room.

"You want to tell us what happened?"

She pointed to the window. "I got home, took a shower, and was changing my clothes. It'd been dark for about an hour. I was getting dressed, drying my hair with a towel. I went to leave the room and turned off the light and pulled the drapes. Then I glanced out the window." She took Dalton's arm and pulled him to the window.

"Right up there, in that gully. See the shadow of the trees? He was right in front of them. Someone was up there smoking a cigarette. I could see the red glow intensify when he'd take a drag. He was watching me."

Dalton pulled her away from the window. "I'll go and check it out. It might be nothing. I mean a beautiful woman walking around naked is going to attract an audience. Maybe some guy was just out on a hike and decided to enjoy the show."

"I'm so embarrassed." Mrs. Devonshire looked at the ceiling. "There didn't used to be other houses around, so I never thought about being watched."

"Don't worry," said Ted.

"By the way, this is Ted, your new bodyguard." Dalton shoved his weapon into its holster. "He goes everywhere you go, until this is finished. You're safe with him in the house."

Outside, Dalton walked along the sidewalk through the neighborhood until he was on the street that over-looked Sophie Devonshire's house. Whoever had been watching her had been stationed up here. He climbed through the weeds of an empty field, stumbling here and there over rocks and gopher holes. Dead weeds crunched beneath his shoes.

There was just enough light to reveal where the ground dropped away and turned into a ravine. Dalton sat and crawled like a spider to reach an area where he could stand upright. This had to be where the man had watched.

He searched the area with his cell-phone flashlight, and found five cigarette butts. He picked up one. It wasn't one of the popular brands. It was a European cigarette, only sold in a few shops in the city. He searched further, found an empty water bottle. Someone had carried water. Their visit was planned. And then Dalton saw something that sent a shiver up his spine. Stuck in a tree branch that was lying on the ground, stood a small knife, its tip wedged deep into the wood, handle pointing up. It was a message. Someone wanted him to find the knife.

CHAPTER 14

Commander Rossi stood on the narrow balcony overlooking Long Beach. In the distance was the *Queen Mary*, a fence of huge stones surrounding it. Out beyond the harbor, where the city lights danced on the black water, monster cranes towered over a field of containers.

The commander turned and stepped into the apartment. Several men were sitting at a long conference table. Another one moved about the photos hanging on the wall, and read the notes attached to them.

"Gentlemen, I received word from Europe. The Key has been traced to Mr. Devonshire. He was at the conference in Cologne when we missed the courier. The only other possibility was that Russian doctor. What was his name? But he was eliminated as a suspect. You took care of that. Right, Uri?"

Uri Dent set down his knife and fork and wiped his mouth with a linen napkin. He cleared his throat and looked at the commander. "Yes, sir. Professor Urtsen was his name. He was eliminated in Chicago. He did not have the Key."

The commander nodded and walked around the table. When he reached the end of the table, he stopped. "I got orders this morning to take the gloves off. His Eminence wants this completed as quickly as possible. We have seven days to complete our mission. If it's not completed in that time, we are not to return to our homes. Europe will be off-limits to every man here."

CHAPTER 15

It was past midnight by the time Dalton returned. The office was as empty as a dancehall on Sunday morning. His steps made a strange hollow sound as he walked to the desk. From the bottom drawer, he took out a bottle of bourbon and poured two fingers into a glass, took a drink, and made his whiskey face. At the sofa he set the glass on the floor, plopped himself down, took off his jacket, and pulled it over himself as he stretched out.

But then he started thinking about Ted and Jax, and the days when the three of them were thick as thieves in high school. Everything had been new and thrilling. He tried to drift off into sleep, but it was no use. Having Ted around, and having seen Jax's new house, made him want to reach out and touch them, to be around them and remember the laughter and the dances, the Friday nights munching popcorn at the drive-in, the speaker hooked on the driver's window. He laughed about Ted's old Pontiac and how the windows kept fogging up. Every few minutes Ted had jumped out and wiped the windshield.

Dalton gave up on sleep and walked to his desk and turned on the computer. He didn't need to do a search to find the site he was looking for. Over the years he'd been there many times. It was where he went to touch the past, to ground himself. On the home page he typed the year he had graduated, and his high school yearbook opened. The faces took him back to morning English class, friends shoving notes into his hand while the teacher was at the chalkboard. Each name, each photograph, brought back a memory. All the browsing, the flipping through the pages, was leading to one thing. After some time with his buddies, he could wait no longer and went to the photo of cheerleader Jax, pom-poms held high.

That night of the photo was their first spent together. Staring into her eyes, sparkling with erotic joy, changed the way he thought about the world, and his place in it.

Dalton didn't know how much bourbon he drank. He didn't look at the clock. This journey had nothing to do with life outside. He was alone in the computers bubble of light. And he slept on the keyboard.

* * *

"Oh no, boss, you didn't sleep like that, did you?" Nick said, waking Dalton as he locked the door behind him, pushing his shoulder bag out of the way, holding a Starbucks carry tray in one hand. He rushed across the room and set the tray on the desk, and pulled the blinds open. The moan of traffic, distant horns, doors slamming, people shouting hellos, entered the office as though carried with the sunlight.

Dalton sat up and rubbed his face and leaned back in his chair. He slowly looked around the room, squinting.

"What are you doing here?" He reached for the Venti size coffee, pulled the top off, and put the paper container to his lips.

Nick took the napkins out of the carrier and wiped up the spilled whiskey from the desk, twisted the top back onto the bourbon bottle, and shoved it in the bottom drawer.

"You have to see this." Nick opened his laptop and started typing. "We finished those papers and found a whole bunch of good stuff. You have to see this."

"Okay. Coffee. I'm glad you brought coffee. Let me wash my face." Dalton stood up and grabbed the edge of the desk and walked to the bathroom.

Nick followed with the laptop. "Remember those listening devices? Someone has been passing your information to a Major Thomas Trenton Gregory."

Dalton leaned over the sink and splashed water over his face and hair. "That's good work. So, someone has hired this Gregory to take me out?"

"That's what it looks like."

Dalton wiped his face with a towel and crossed the office. "You always bring such pleasant news."

"That's what I'm good at."

Dalton sipped his coffee. "Strong coffee is the only thing that gets me out of bed."

"Or off the desk."

"You really have your smartass going. How many energy drinks did you slurp down last night?"

"Maybe a few, after a few."

"That's way too much caffeine. But you got a name. That means we can track him. Maybe it's time to spin the table on this Gregory guy. What else did you get?"

"That Mr. Devonshire was one sneaky dude." Nick pulled a poster-board from his bag, unfolded it on the desk, and searched while moving a finger over the surface. "Here it is. The house that Sophie mentioned is actually two houses."

"How is that possible?"

"Because they own the one, and a shell corporation owns the second."

"And Mr. Devonshire owns the shell corporation."

"Exactly."

"And the houses are beside each other?"

"Yes."

"That's the perfect way to make sure your neighbors don't get nosy."

Nick laughed and straightened up. "Holy crap, I need to crash."

"Sleep on the sofa. Good work. You're going to need the rest.

We have a lot of legwork coming up."

* * *

They hadn't been in the car for more than a few minutes before Nick looked around and asked: "Where we going? This isn't the way the San Pedro."

"I want to check something at the Hall of Records. They should have a record of the house. I want to check the floor plan. The county will have a record."

The county registrar, where all real-estate records for LA County were kept, was in one of the busiest sections of Norwalk. In front of the hall ran a six-lane boulevard between two of LA's busiest freeways.

The parking lot of the Hall of Records had turned into a place of business. The main pedestrian corridor out of the parking lot was filled with people selling legal forms and the services of a notary public. A visitor could get married and file a property lien the same day.

After wading through a line and speaking to the public service agent behind the glass, and then paying a fee, Dalton was given access to the property records for the address in San Pedro.

As a clerk turned over the records and pointed to a computer terminal, he asked about the address once more, and called to another agent working two windows away. When the other agent heard the name of the street, he climbed down off his stool, and walked to Dalton's window.

He read the address and smiled. "Yeah, I grew up on Daisy, the next street over. But all of the kids spent their time on Petaluma."

"Why is that?"

"That's where the fort was. There used to be a couple of underground warehouses on Petaluma. The other kids and I converted one into our clubhouse." He smiled and stood up straight.

"Rumor was they belonged to a dairy farmer. Back when he stored his cheese there."

"What happened to them?"

"That's a good question. Now it's just houses out there. The city must have torn them out, filled them up when I was in the military. That's what I always thought."

Dalton thanked the guy and sat down at a computer terminal. He flipped through the house blueprints, and detail page that showed the yard.

"This is strange." Dalton drummed his fingers on the desk. "How old do you think that guy is?"

Nick glanced to the civil servants behind the windows.

"I'm guessing he's in his early sixties. That would've put him playing in that neighborhood in the 1960s. But these plans are dated 1982. I'm guessing that somebody, possibly Mr. Devonshire, paid a handsome sum to make the warehouse plans disappear."

"Why did Mr. Devonshire need a secret warehouse? What's he hiding?"

Dalton turned off the computer. "It's time to find out. You up for a drive?"

"Well, yeah." Nick typed something on his cell phone and looked up. "That's where we set out to go, right?"

Dalton snatched Nick's phone. "Tell me you didn't just text about what we found to one of your computer buddies."

Nick drew his head back. "No. No way. Boss. I would never say anything about the case."

"Who did you text? Tell me or I'll smash it."

"Ah!" Nick walked away and came back quickly. "It's just this girl. She wants to meet, okay?"

Dalton returned the cheap phone. "Don't tell her about Bugsy."

"That again?"

* * *

The house sat back from the street and was surrounded by a spongy, thick lawn of Bermuda grass. Close to the house, the half circle driveway passed a dry fountain filled with dead leaves. Sitting on a street of Spanish-style homes built in the forties, the fountain house looked more like a small library or museum.

Dalton parked beside the fountain, hopped up the front steps, and tried the brass door handle. It refused to move. He pushed several times, then gave up and leaned forward and peeked through the crack between curtain and door frame.

Nick thumped on the wall with a hand. "Is this stone? I don't think I've ever seen a house built of stone in California."

"They used to be everywhere," said Dalton. "An earthquake in 1933 knocked down most of them." He hurried around the side of the house, trying windows as he went. "Mrs. Devonshire said that there would be a key on this ledge." Dalton reached over the side gate and found the key.

They pushed open the gate. It scraped the concrete walkway, and they walked around the back of the house to the rear door. Behind the house stood a massive oak tree with a dangling swing. The rear door was made of quarter-sawn oak, with beveled glass in the side windows and a speakeasy door at eye level. Dalton fiddled with the skeleton key for a few minutes and finally managed to get the lock to click open. The door was another matter. He pushed several times but it didn't move. Then he put his shoulder against it and shoved.

When it gave way, it flew open and he barged into a spacious kitchen. Old maroon and yellow tile covered the countertops and floor. "Man," he said, pulling the curtains away from the window. "I wonder how long it's been since sunlight got in here."

They moved from room to room, touching photographs of the Devonshire family at different times of the year. Each photo was in its own little frame, covered with dust. The bedroom contained images from the couple's youth, where the couple looked like teenagers, and in the adjacent rooms the couple in the photos aged, as though each room contained part of their life.

Dalton searched books, opened the medicine cabinet, read old mail, and looked for the reason Mr. Devonshire had spent so much time here.

"Hey," called Nick. "You better get in here."

Dalton hurried out of the bedroom, down the creaking hallway, and into the living room. The dining table had been shoved against the wall, and the rug was bunched up beside it. A trap door in the floor stood open, and Nick was halfway down the stairs.

"Be careful. We don't know what's down there."

Nick leaned over and looked beneath the floorboards, down into the basement. "It does look pretty creepy. You don't think there's spiders, do you?"

"It's a basement. That's spider world."

"I hate you." Nick climbed up.

"Maybe it's what we're looking for."

Dalton took out his automatic and climbed down.

The basement looked like the vault room of a bank. The walls were concrete blocks painted a gloss mustard. The floor was coated with a clear epoxy that held black and white flecks beneath a surface that appeared wet. A carved teak desk sat against the back wall. And behind the desk, a cork bulletin board covered the wall. Pinned to the bulletin board with colored pins were newspaper clippings, maps and photographs, drawings of lands with biblical names.

Nick went to a heavy metal door in one of the walls and tried the lock. "Did she tell you where the key was for this?"

"I don't think she's ever been down here."

Among the papers on the bulletin board, Dalton found an advertisement for the seminar in Germany and put his finger on it. "This is where it began. Look at this."

Nick glanced at the ceiling and pulled his collar tight around his neck.

"Forget about the spiders. Look. He has the names of all the speakers at that seminar." Dalton moved his hand down the list. "Every one of them has died, and Mr. Devonshire was keeping track."

"Oh, here we go." Dalton removed a photograph of a dead man. Paper clipped to it was a newspaper article that mentioned a Special Forces unit attached to the Vatican.

"Oh, look who gets mentioned."

"The Vatican?"

"Yes. Rossi and his men are tracking the artifact, working their way down the list of attendees."

Nick shook his head. "Why would they be killing people?"

"They want the map and the treasure." Dalton stuck the photo back on the board and moved through the basement. "Look at this place. Everything has been modernized: electrical conduit new and shiny, bright new lights everywhere, new paint. But look at the desk. That thing must have been built in the 1920s. The rug, the desk lamp, the chair beside the desk, they're all old." He touched the desk.

"Mr. Devonshire loved old things, but liked to be comfortable, too."

"Yeah, that's what I'm thinking." Dalton sat at the desk.

"So, what do we do now?"

"There's always something that doesn't fit. That's what you have to look for. What do you see in this room that doesn't fit?"

"That door," said Nick, pointing at the wide metal door. "It should be on some castle in Scotland."

"It has to be this chair. We know the guy came here alone. Why are there two chairs at the desk? He has a chair for himself, but why is the other one here?" Dalton stood up and tilted the chair back. He reached down and touched a metal ornament that protruded from the front of each leg. Across the room, he noticed two marks scratched in the metal door. Then he turned the chair over. Stuck to the bottom on a metal brace was a magnetic key box. He smiled. "It's good you have a master detective with you."

"How'd you know?"

"It doesn't fit. This was the last place he wanted a visitor, right? If the warehouse is hidden here, I'm guessing that a man who dealt in antiquities has some pretty nice pieces stashed away."

Dalton removed the box, slid open the top, and removed a skeleton key.

"Now *that's* a key," laughed Nick.

Dalton walked to the metal door.

"Are you sure we want to go in? With a door like that, it's got to be major creepy inside."

Dalton turned the key in the lock. The door opened with a long creak. He took out his flashlight cell phone, and looked around inside. It didn't take them long to find the light switch.

"Oh my God," said Dalton.

The old warehouse was about 300 square feet. In one corner stood three Greek statues, a sofa between them. In the center of the room stood a wall of plywood six feet tall. On it hung two paintings.

"That's a Van Gogh. That can't be authentic." Nick walked to the paintings and looked them over. "This was lost during World War II." He swiped a finger across the screen of his phone, and read: "*Painter on the Road to Tarascon,* it is called."

"Is this a Degas?" Dalton leaned forward and touched a brass plaque on the frame of the other painting.

"Don't touch!" Nick shoved him. "That's *Five Dancing Women.* That was my art teacher's favorite painting."

"These two paintings must be worth millions. Crap. Don't touch anything! This just turned into a sand trap."

Nick shoved his phone into a pocket. "What are you talking about?"

"Look around. This wasn't one eccentric collector. Two world-class paintings stashed away has to mean an organization. To find these paintings, to move them without the authorities finding out, in and out of countries, moving payments around without alerting the tax authorities, that takes major power."

"Okay, so what's–"

"Did you touch anything? Anything at all?" Dalton pulled his shirt from his waistband, and wiped the plaque on the painting that he'd touched. "What's the big deal? We have to get out of here. Come on." They backed up a few steps, turned and headed to the door. "Think it through, Nick. A group with that kind of power can't leave two paintings like that lying around. They'll be exposed. We don't want to be around when they send in the clean-up crew."

"What about Solomon's Key?"

"I think it's here. There's something bugging me. I'm not seeing something."

"Then keep looking."

"This isn't a place to hang around. We could die here. Don't mention this basement or the paintings to anyone; not Ted, not your mom, not even that girl you're texting with."

"We're just going to have coffee." Nick shook his head.

Dalton stopped at a steamer trunk with a rounded top and shiny brass hinges, like a pirate's treasure chest. He tried the latch and made a noise of surprise inside his throat when he found it was not locked. The top opened unevenly and got stuck, until Nick came over and they both pulled it open.

"Holy shit," said Nick, and jumped back.

Stacks of crisp hundred-dollar bills, Swiss francs, and Euros filled the trunk. Each currency was wrapped in a block covered with clear plastic. Each block was the size of a small suitcase.

Nick gasped and reached out a hand. "Can I take one home, or touch it? Can I touch it? Let me just talk to it."

"Here, let's take them to show Mrs. Devonshire. Don't touch the trunk."

Nick lifted the blocks.

Dalton closed the trunk and pulled off his shirt and wiped their fingerprints from the lid. "Someone has to know about that money. Stacks of cash and the owner died. That's an invitation to get the money."

Nick looked around the warehouse. "If this trunk has cash in it, what do you suppose is in that one?" He pointed at another trunk, four feet away.

"I'm afraid to look."

Dalton opened the second trunk. Wrapped in plastic was the body of a man. Areas of his face had liquefied, as though they had melted, exposing the skull. One eye ball hung from the socket, and the lips had long since turned to brown liquid, exposing fillings in his teeth.

"Oh, fuck." Nick jumped away and turned his back.

"Come on, let's get out of here."

Dalton wiped everything they'd touched. Back upstairs, they went through every room, wiping every photograph, every doorknob, each light switch. Before they stepped outside, Dalton covered the blocks of cash with his shirt.

CHAPTER 16

Dalton climbed into the car and looked around. "Man, what is it with you and old cars? You've been driving around in junk cars ever since high school."

"What do you mean, junk cars? This is a 1967 Chevy Malibu. It's a classic. Thank you very much."

Dalton flipped down the sun visor and bounced up and down on the black seat. "Why don't you walk into a dealership like a normal person and buy a new car? I'll bet that if I opened the trunk right now, I'd find a toolbox full of tools you need to keep this thing on the road."

"Oh." Ted nodded several times and grabbed the steering wheel with both hands. "I got tools, okay? Things happen. It's a classic car. I like driving cars from the sixties. If you don't like it, you can get out and catch a bus."

"I'm just saying, first it was that old Pontiac. You had to grab the windows and pull them up with your hands to roll them up. And then you had the Monte Carlo. It burned so much oil that people were always throwing things and telling you to get off the road."

"Did you want to meet so you could insult my automobiles?"

Dalton laughed. "No, I just needed to talk. We really fell into it at the San Pedro house."

"Is anyone following you?" Ted reached under his coat for his weapon while checking the mirrors.

"No, we stayed a step ahead of them. I think Mr. Devonshire was a big-time player in black market art."

"Why? What'd you find?"

"A body. He had a trunk with a body stuffed in it. And get this: twin trunks, one with a body, and the other filled with currency wrapped and stacked like in a bank vault."

Ted looked over. "No! Money like that means big-time bad people. That amount of green don't sit around without people knowing about it. And now with the big dawg gone, they're gunna come sniffing."

"Exactly."

"We get out, right?"

"I can't leave Sophie like that."

"Yes, you can. Money like that means a ruthless organization. We just move along before they put bullet holes in us."

"She needs our help."

"And that's Dalton in a nut shell: always trying to help some woman."

Ted checked his mirrors, shifted into first gear, and rolled out onto Gaffey street, heading toward the bridge over the harbor, back into Long Beach.

As they drove, Dalton remembered the old down town around city hall, the park, the brass cannon, and the old library with its creaky floor. He preferred his childhood memories of the area to what he saw now: abandoned crack houses, restaurants all crammed onto a few streets like covered wagons grouping together.

Ted exited the freeway and turned up Ocean Boulevard where formula 1 cars in the Grand Prix had left burned tire marks. A few blocks east of Alamitos Boulevard, the city disappeared on the ocean side. A cliff dropped to the sand where a bike path followed the beach. Along the path strolled couples, joggers, and business-men and women talking into headsets. And past it all was the Pacific Ocean, glimmering in the setting sun. On the horizon sat Catalina Island, a dark spot in the distance, a few clouds hovering above.

Ted turned on to Redondo and tapped Dalton on the arm. "Hey, I think we got a tail. That Lexus back there has been with me since I got off the freeway."

"Okay, let's see what they got. Take a right." Dalton pointed and glanced over his shoulder.

One block before Broadway, Ted turned onto a residential street.

An Army truck that was coming toward them, crossed into their lane and blocked the street. The Lexus skidded to a halt behind them. The doors burst open, and the woman from the diner jumped out with several associates.

Dalton turned.

Uri Dent climbed out of the Lexus, along with two men.

Uri walked over and tapped on Ted's window.

"Step away from the vehicle," shouted the woman. "These are my prisoners. I will not say it again." She shouted something in Hebrew, and her associates aimed automatic weapons.

"Relax," said Uri Dent, holding his hands in the air and walking backward, away from the Malibu.

One of Uri's men shouted and dropped behind Ted's car and fired three shots. The first shot knocked one of the Israeli men off his feet.

"Oh, fuck this, I ain't getting killed!" Ted shoved the gear-shift into reverse, turned and looked over the seat as he stomped on the gas. He smashed into the Lexus and kept going, pushing the vehicle along the street.

"Come on!" shouted Ted. The rear wheels of the Malibu were smoking as they spun; the engine screamed as it pushed the Lexus up the curb. The moment the Lexus hopped up the curb, Ted shoved the gear-shift into first. The Malibu had just begun to roll forward when several shots tore into the fender, and the tire exploded.

Dalton shouted and pulled the door handle. But his door didn't open. He shouted again and threw his shoulder against the door several times. The fourth time he hit the door, it opened and he jumped out.

"We don't have anything," he shouted, holding his hands over his head and jumping about in the street. "Stop shooting! Whatever it is you're looking for, we don't have it. What the fuck! We just need to go on our way, all right? I'm trying to earn a living. I'm an investigator. I don't have what you're looking for, so get the fuck out of the street and stop shooting."

"You don't have the artifact?" asked one of the Italian agents. He raised up on his elbows where he lay in the grass.

"And you, you crazy bitch." Dalton ran at the Israeli truck, took out his weapon, swung it like a hammer, and shattered the passenger window.

"Hell no." Ted grabbed his arm and pulled him backward. "Put your weapon away! Are you out of your mind? You're going to get us killed. You got shooters on both sides, you idiot."

Dalton tripped and they fell to the warm asphalt.

"Okay," shouted one of the Italians. "We are putting down our weapons."

The Israeli woman shouted, and the short, heavyset man, who was kneeling behind a tree, set down his weapon and sprinted to Dalton and Ted; he quickly frisked them. After he had searched their pockets and patted them down, he threw his hands into the air and stood up. "I got nothing," he said.

Before the Israeli had finished searching, one of the Italians ran to the Malibu and rifled through it. He dumped the contents of the glovebox on the floor, dug fast-food wrappers from beneath the seat, and emptied a cloth shopping bag into the street. "Nothing here, either," he shouted.

"My car! Those fuckers shot my car!" After he had circled the Malibu a couple of times and whimpered every time he touched a dent or bullet hole, Ted opened the trunk. "Now I'm going to take my toolbox out and change the tire! Because I have a toolbox, I can at least change my tire."

"Drop me at my car, would ya? I need to drive my normal-person car."

Ted threw the lug wrench into the street. "You motherfucker. I pick you up and my car gets beaten to hell and shot up, and now it ain't good enough for you to drive in?"

"I got to go back to that basement and get rid of those paintings."

"Whoa, you can't go back there. There's a body in there. If you take those paintings, that's interfering with a criminal investigation." Ted leaned forward and slapped his thighs.

"I know."

"Dalton, you could do time for that. You don't have to help that woman."

"Look, those paintings are going to make headlines, and it's all going to be linked to her husband. That's a hard spotlight to bear."

Ted sat on the curb and picked up the lug wrench. He looked one way and then the other, and then up at Dalton. "Either you go in there with a full body suit and a hairnet and something dragging behind you that doesn't leave one single fragment of a footprint, or you go the other direction and drive a herd of elephants through that basement and make it impossible for investigators to find any clue, any piece of evidence."

Dalton held up his cell phone and shook it. "That gives me an idea. Why don't you head back to the office and try not to shoot Nick? I'll get back as quick as I can."

"What are you going to do?"

"I want to make sure they get into the right hands."

Dalton called Uber and got a ride to his car. On the way, he thought about his plan. All he had to do was drive out to the basement in San Pedro and grab a couple paintings. But these weren't any paintings. There wasn't a king or billionaire anywhere who wouldn't give a lot and go out of his way to own one.

But first he had a little research to do. After twenty minutes on a library computer, he had written down the phone numbers he needed. Once he had those, he got back in his car, drove up the 405 N. and down the 110 into the South Bay, straight into San Pedro.

It was easy enough to get back into the house, and down into the basement and remove the paintings. He shoved them into the trunk of his car as though he had bought them at some secondhand store. But there was something that troubled him about that basement. Ever since he'd first set foot in there, a little detail was nagging at him: something that his subconscious had seen hadn't registered with his conscious mind yet. He knew it was there, something out of place, something that didn't fit, and the thought that he'd missed something kept chewing at him.

The scam he arranged to get the paintings into the proper hands was another matter. Soon he was heading up the 710 freeway, making his way to Pasadena, and then into San Marino. Once he got into San Marino, he pulled into the nearest Home Depot, and arranged for a migrant worker to help him out.

He pulled into the parking lot of the Huntington Museum, and called for an Uber driver to pick up his helper. Then he dialed the number for the director of the museum.

When the man answered, he said, "Dr. Rosenthal, I'm sending a man up right now who is carrying with him two paintings that I am turning over to your museum."

"This is a most unusual call. How did you get my number?" said the voice on the other end.

"The first painting is *Five Dancing Women*, by Edgar Degas. I have contacted the representatives of Baron Herzog's estate. The Nazis took the painting from him during World War II."

There was a silence at the other end. After a moment, a man came back on and cleared his throat. "If this is some sort of a joke —"

"Dr. Rosenthal, this is not a joke, Sir. If you prefer, I can just as easily bring them to the Getty."

"No, you don't have to do that. I will come out and take a look. What is the second painting?"

"It's a Van Gogh, painted in 1888, *Painter on the Road to Tarascon*."

"Oh, my God. They need to be preserved with special lighting, humidity control. I am coming."

"I've also notified the *Los Angeles Times* that these paintings have been found and are presently being held by your museum until they can be given over to the proper owners."

Dalton paid the worker a hundred bucks, put him in the Uber Prius with the paintings, and sent him up to the museum. He was pulling out of the museum parking lot when he heard his phone, and looked down at the little rinky-dink screen of the throwaway cell. He pulled out of traffic and parked, and read the text: *Ted shot. Memorial Hospital. Be there soon.*

The moment he read that text, he started thinking about the times he was in the jungle on some mission in Central America with Ted. He remembered their days in high school, when he thought he was going to die during football practice, his legs so weak they were shaking from running bleachers and the coach shouting at them to get their asses back up there and keep going. It was always Ted who jumped out in front of the whole team and broke out the Ted dance. It was that dance that made everyone laugh and not think so much about their pain. And Ted was the only one that he trusted to look after Jax.

He knew that now was the perfect time to spin the tables on the Israelis and the Italians. Ted would be happy about it.

Back at the property in San Pedro, Dalton parked the car a couple blocks away from the fountain house, and found a nice bench where he could sit and watch the whole thing go down. Then he got on his cell phone, contacted the commander, and asked for his help investigating what looked like a warehouse that Mr. Devonshire had kept hidden. He made it clear that whatever the Italians found belonged to his client. He tried to be forceful enough to make it sound real. At the end of the conversation, Dalton told him the address of the house with the fountain.

The instant he hung up, he dialed the Israeli crew. And then he sat back and watched. It would've been better with a tub of popcorn, he thought. That would have been perfect, sitting on the park bench, munching away as the crews converged on the house.

Two vehicles pulled up, and men ran about here and there and got in each other's face and shouted. Moments later, four or five of them disappeared into the house.

Dalton knew exactly how long it would take to find the basement hatch, how long it would take them to stomp around in the basement with their boots on, searching through every drawer, knocking things over, tainting every single footprint or hair or bit of evidence that any investigator could ever hope to find. After he waited the perfect amount of time, he dialed 911 and reported men with guns running about the house, speaking a foreign language, and carrying what looked like explosives. His next call went to the fire department, and he reported seeing smoke coming out of the windows.

Yes, Uri Dent had left a knife stuck in a piece of wood behind Sophie Devonshire's house as a message to him. Now Dalton had returned the favor.

He wanted to stay and see the crews arrested, dragged away screaming about diplomatic immunity, but as sirens started to wail in the distance, Dalton got to his feet and walked to his car. He got lucky with traffic and made it to the hospital in record time.

* * *

At the hospital, he wound his way down one corridor and turned up another. Nurses hurried past. Some of them carried clipboards and shuffled through papers as they walked. One or two pushed electronic devices on carts. A couple of EMTs pushed a gurney. Up ahead he saw Nick leaning against the wall, his head tilted back, staring at the ceiling.

"What happened? Is he going to be okay?"

Nick looked at him. His shirt was smeared with blood. There was blood on his cheek.

"Oh, man. I heard the shots and tried to get down to him as quick as I could. He kept repeating the name Gregory."

"Is he going to live? That's what I want to know."

"The doctor is operating now."

"Okay. You made a file on that guy, Thomas Trenton Gregory, right?"

"Yeah, it's back in the office." Nick suddenly looked angry. "Look boss. If you're going to go visit that Gregory bastard, I want to be there."

"No Nick, I have to go underground for a while. I need you at the fort, okay?"

"That's what my dad used to say when he'd go hunting."

Dalton nodded. "Well, I am going hunting."

He got half way down the corridor when he heard a woman asking for directions. The voice stopped him. He'd imagined it so many times, he didn't know if he was actually hearing it.

"Martin is the patient's last name, Ted Martin."

Jax was wrapped in a wool jacket that reached her thighs, and black leather boots that nearly touched the bottom of the jacket. Her wavy blonde hair was pulled back in a baby-blue beanie that matched the big fluffy scarf wrapped around her neck. Her cheeks had a red tint to them.

The nurse she was trying to communicate with was speaking Spanish to an elderly couple, and held up her hand to stop Jax. After she said goodbye to the couple, she spoke in English.

"Mr. Martin," she said. "I believe he's down the hall in room number six. He's pretty heavily sedated. He just got out of surgery, but it looks like he's going to be fine."

Dalton turned to the wall. He wanted to walk back the way that he had come. He also wanted to reach out to Jax. He stepped one direction, then stopped and turned to go the other.

"Uncle," said Nick, seeing Jax and realizing what was happening. "Here, let me help you." Nick put his arm around Dalton and led him down the hallway, away from Jax.

"She's here." Dalton looked over his shoulder and pointed once they reached the main lobby. "How'd she find out about Ted?"

CHAPTER 17

It was one of those rare overcast days in Los Angeles. A breeze moved the palms about and was just cool enough to make everyone remember winter. Flower trucks were still on the streets delivering white buckets of gladiolas and roses to the corner stands, when Dalton rolled off the freeway and into the big city. A city truck was parked in the street beside a bus stop, and a worker in waders was pressure washing the bus-stop. A few homeless men had woken up and were shuffling along the sidewalk, when Dalton pulled into the parking garage underneath one of the downtown high-rises. He drove around beneath low concrete supports until he found a parking space. He hadn't yet locked his car door when a security guard approached and asked the nature of his visit.

A blonde woman with her hair pulled up and her neckline pulled low, met him at the elevator with an iPad. He followed her down the corridor, past large conference rooms encased in glass, and into an office.

Sophie Devonshire looked very different here. Her hair was done up on top of her head. The tiny dress she was wearing said business, but made it clear that she was a shapely, attractive woman. She turned from the floor-to-ceiling windows that provided a breath-taking view of the city.

"Mr. Dalton, I'm so glad that you came down." She waved to a leather chair.

Dalton walked over and sat down. "Mrs. Devonshire, Sophie, I have some unpleasant business that I need to discuss."

"Okay. In that case, let me make sure that we have the room completely to ourselves." She went to the door and pushed the stop out from beneath it. Once it swung to, she checked to see that it was locked, walked around behind her desk, and pressed a button on the telephone. "Sadie, please see that I'm not disturbed for the next hour," she said.

She hung up the phone and sat beside Dalton.

"I got into your house in San Pedro," he said. "How long has it been since you were in that house?"

Sophie Devonshire rubbed her hands together. "Oh, my goodness, I guess it's been ages. I can't remember the last time I was there with my husband. Years, I would say. Why?"

Dalton watched her face closely and noticed the movement of her eyes each time he asked her a question. "Your husband was definitely living in a secret life."

"Women? Did he have another woman?" Sophie's face turned red, and she looked at the ceiling.

"No, I don't believe he did. Your husband was involved in stolen art. It looks like he was a member of a black-market operation. Do you know anything about that?"

She drew back. "Jason, I need you to lay it out for me, please. You are not talking about one or two stamps, right?"

Dalton repositioned himself on the chair. "No. I found paintings that went missing during World War II. The value of those paintings alone is well over twenty million dollars."

Sophie Devonshire jumped to her feet and paced from the window to the door. She tried to speak several times, but no sound came from her throat.

"If either one of those paintings are exposed to the art world, it would be international news," he said.

She stopped at the window and stood staring out over the city. "I know my husband loved art and beautiful things. He just couldn't live his life without feeling the joy that art brought him. But this—"

"I'm sorry to say, there's more."

Sophie walked back to the chair, reached down and felt the arm, and remained standing as though lost in thought. "Tell me," she said. "I'm ready for the rest of it. That's what I paid you for."

"Are you sure you want to hear this?"

She sat down in the chair and placed her hands on her knees, and looked at him. "I have to know. There's no way around it. What did you find?"

Dalton shook his head yes, and wiped a finger across his lips as he looked at a decanter filled with an amber-colored liquid. "Is that whiskey?" he asked.

"Oh, yes, but not just whiskey. That's eighteen-year-old bourbon. And this is the perfect time for it." Sophie got up and pulled the top out; she poured a couple fingers of the liquid into two classes. Before she turned, she drank the contents of one of the glasses and refilled it.

"Did you burn yourself?" he asked, and touched her arm where a dark imperfection marred the skin.

She looked. "Oh, no, it's a birth mark."

Dalton threw back half the whiskey. It was so smooth, he wished he had drunk the other half at the same time.

"That's good bourbon." He set his glass down and looked at Mrs. Devonshire. "We found a body."

Sophie jumped to her feet and emptied her glass. She waved a hand through the air and said, "A body? You found a body at the house in San Pedro? A dead person? Oh, my God!"

"We also found about three million in cash, Swiss francs, Euros, and US dollars."

"That's death money. My God, I don't want to touch that money. If those paintings disappeared during World War II, that means they were taken from Jewish families. That is horrible." She pulled the pin from her hair, and it fell down her back. She shook it loose, poured more whiskey, kicked off her high heels, and dropped into the seat once more.

"You had no idea what was going on?"

"No idea. What am I going to do, Jason?"

"I made sure the paintings got to their proper owners. Otherwise, having a body there with the paintings would be a story way too intriguing for the media to pass up. It's still going to blow up, but to a much smaller degree."

Sophie stretched her legs. "Thank you. I think that will take a lot of pressure off the situation."

"And you're going to contact one of the best criminal attorneys in the country."

Sophie picked up her drink.

Dalton stood up and took it out of her hand. "No," he said. "You need to be thinking clearly. Right now, you can get out ahead of this. Contact your attorney, and he'll begin the proceedings."

Dalton stayed with her for about an hour, talking her through it, getting her ready for the questioning and the spotlight that was about to be shone on her life.

CHAPTER 18

They parked behind the building with the other tenants' cars, and walked around to the front entrance. Dalton reached into his pocket and took out his keys as they approached the landing.

"It smells like an Indian restaurant up here."

"Is that curry?"

The instant Dalton opened the door and stepped into the office, the full smell of the cooking hit him.

"Oh, my friends," called Mr. Singh with that Indian accent, as he rushed across the office.

"What are you doing here, Singh? Why are you making food in my office?"

The smile left Mr. Singh's face as he shook a wooden spoon in the air. "It is only my rice cooker and wok. I am Indian. I have to have good food, not that crap you Americans eat, hamburgers and hotdogs. I would've been dead long ago had I not known from the first day I landed in this country that what you call 'food' is merely a formula to put you in an early grave. That is why I make curries, the best in the world, the way my mother taught me to make them." He turned and walked to the rice cooker.

"Singh, you're in my office. This isn't your apartment. What are you doing here?"

Nick walked over to the cooking food. "How long before that

stuff is done?"

"I know I told you I would go back to India. I was praying all the way to the airport. I must have prayed the same prayer hundreds of times, and then it came to me: Mr. Dalton, this isn't just some artifact dug up in the desert somewhere. If the treasure of Solomon's mines is as vast as everyone believes, it could change history. I want to be part of that."

"Listen, a friend of mine was shot tonight. All I want to think about right now is finding this Gregory guy that shot him."

"I would be doing the same you're doing, Mr. Dalton. But you have to look at the bigger picture. Your friend was only one man. What you need to be doing, what the three of us need to be doing, is searching for Solomon's Key."

Nick picked up the wooden spoon and stirred the vegetables simmering in the wok. "If we find that artifact, all these bad guys will just disappear. And then we hit Costco and buy everything we ever wanted, right?"

"Nick, where is that file that you started on Gregory?"

Mr. Singh walked over to Nick's table and picked up a file. "I found this file and did some digging before you two gentlemen returned. That is what I do best: I spend twelve hours a day digging around online, doing research, and have developed excellent digging skills. This Mr. Gregory that you mentioned, works out of a run-down commercial building downtown."

Nick hurried over and picked up the file and read. "Whoa, Singh, that's pretty good research! Maybe we should keep you around for a while."

"The first thing in the morning, I'm going to go on a little hunting expedition. And like I told Nick before, I need you both to stay here while I'm gone. You're not going to hear from me, okay? As soon as I get back, we'll finish tracking down the Key. Nick, while I'm gone I need you to prepare a list of possibilities, where Devonshire may have stored that thing. I need safety deposit boxes, storage facilities, rented apartments or houses, anything. Let's finish this."

Mr. Singh scooped up a helping of rice onto a paper plate,

added some of the vegetables and curry. "Okay, Mr. Nick, this first one is for you."

Nick took the plate and moved it in a circle under his nose. "Oh, boy, that smells good."

"And when you come back from your little expedition, Mr. Dalton, we should drive out to that underground warehouse in San Pedro. That sounds like the most promising place to hide the Key."

"How did you find out about that, Singh?"

"How did I find out? I found the list of the Devonshire properties here on Mr. Nick's desk. He had drawn a star beside the property in San Pedro, and that made me curious, so I drove out to the Hall of Records and made some inquiries. Anyone with brains could have done the same thing."

Dalton sacked out on the sofa.

※ ※ ※

Sometime in the night, after the traffic noise faded away, the glass in the front door shattered. Dime-size pieces of glass flew into the office and scattered across the floor as though a child had dropped a bag of marbles. Dalton jumped up from the desk with his 9 mm in his hand, but the sight of six men wearing FBI jackets, all pointing shotguns, took away all thought of pulling the trigger.

"Okay, I'm putting the weapon down."

The lights snapped on, and into the office walked a clean-cut man in his late thirties. His blonde hair was cut so short on the sides that you could see his scalp. Up on top his hair was long and covered with an oil that made it shine. His head snapped right and left as he shouted orders and strutted across the office, shoving a Beretta into his shoulder holster. "Jason Dalton, I have a warrant to search your office and to take you into custody," he announced.

The agents shoved Dalton to the ground. One held a shotgun barrel to his head, while another clamped handcuffs on his wrists. They left him there on the cold tile floor.

"Well if it isn't the feds. Did you get all heartbroken because I insulted Agent Lowenthal?"

"No," said the blonde. "I'm here to arrest a murderer. You're being charged with murder one."

Dalton rolled onto his side and struggled to sit up. He managed to get up on one knee and then to stand. He looked around the office for Nick and Singh, but they were gone.

Agents collected Nick's laptop and all the files that they could pack into boxes. One of them kicked the wok out of the way, and sent it sliding across the floor.

"And who am I supposed to have killed?"

"Agent Howard Morbund, who we found stuffed in a trunk in San Pedro. Does that ring any bells?"

"And who are you? Where is Lowenthal? Did he eat too much to get out of bed this morning?"

"I'm Agent Trent. My superiors sent me from DC to take over this investigation. It seems Mr. Morbund, or Agent Morbund, was at one time in charge of the Arts Crime Unit. And we found two nice clean prints on the trunk the body was found in. Do you care to guess whose prints they were?"

✻ ✻ ✻

In between his lawyer visit, and waiting to be arraigned, Dalton had a lot of time to think. There in the holding cell, with inmates pacing around, whispering to one another, guards shouting down the corridor, keys rattling, electronic switches being triggered to open cells, he thought over the chain of events that had led him here. The case had bitten him. But how, he wondered, did it spin a hundred and eighty degrees? Dalton remembered being in the basement, starting at one corner of the trunk and wiping it down thoroughly, removing any trail from himself to the dead body. There were no prints there. He knew that. The only possible explanation was that someone had entered the basement after him, and planted his prints.

❊ ❊ ❊

Eventually, two FBI agents came walking down the corridor, escorted by the police jailer. They opened the door and told Dalton to turn around so they could clamp on the handcuffs. He was led through the station and down several corridors, up a flight of stairs. He almost laughed when they opened an interrogation room door and shoved him inside, because it looked like the interrogation room used in every cop show he'd ever seen. In the center stood a wooden table that was bolted to the floor. Across the table was a metal bar they clamped his handcuffs to. On the wall facing the table was a large mirror.

This wasn't normal. Dalton knew that. Prisoners were not taken and interrogated without their attorney unless national security was at stake. Word of those bundles of cash he had found must have reached people in high positions. The paintings were mixed up in the whole mess too, the mess he walked into when he took the case. But now the paintings were out of the picture. He had taken care of that. But cash had a way of changing loyalties and ethical boundaries for cops and civilians alike. Knowing where a large amount of cash was…well, that was as tempting as the drop dead gorgeous woman who whispers in your ear as she sets her room key on the bar and pushes it in your direction.

Dalton didn't know how this was going to go. He didn't think they could pound on him or slowly torture him for answers, not in a police station. That would have to be done somewhere off the books. He would disappear during a transfer, or a faked breakout would be staged for the benefit of the press.

Then they'd be able to work on him. Nonetheless, Dalton sat up straight, placed his feet firmly on the floor, and got himself ready for the worst.

In the Army he had seen interrogations done thousands of times. He'd also been trained in how to survive one. The secret to disrupting an interrogation was as simple as replaying a song. He'd just keep one song playing in his head and sing it when he needed to. That was the easiest way in the world not to get caught up in all the stress and fear and panic that the interrogator was trying to inflict to get the information he wanted.

He didn't have to worry about his story, because the only thing he was going to say was the magic phrase: *I want a lawyer.* That would be his response to every single question they were going to ask, regardless. If he felt intimidated or afraid, he'd just keep repeating it.

The only thing he needed now was a song he could keep going back to. And there really wasn't any choice. It was an oldie that had been playing the first night he had slept with Jax: Me and Bobby McGee" by Janis Joplin. As soon as the lyrics started playing in his head, he started tapping his fingers on the table, remembering that night, remembering the smile in her eyes. And that made him laugh. Even though he was handcuffed to a table, part of Dalton had left the room.

The door opened and an overweight cop who was trying to suck in his gut to keep it from hanging over his belt, carried in a Styrofoam cup of coffee and set it on the table. Beside it he dropped a folder filled with papers.

"You're going down for this one, Dalton. We got your fingerprints on a trunk with a dead body in it. Not even going to offer you a deal. You're going to do hard time, and the boys up there are going to pay you some special attention."

Dalton smiled and tapped rhythm on the table and stared at the wall past the guy who was trying so hard to loom large and fearsome in front of him. In a soft voice he sang, "From the Kentucky coal mines, to the California sun…"

He was holding all the cards. He knew that. The only reason

he was in that room was because he had something they wanted. And the farther that room was from the main interrogation rooms, the farther hidden away he was, the more they wanted what he had.

The cop leaned down close to Dalton. "What the fuck did you just say?"

"I said I want my lawyer."

"People in hell want ice water, boy, but they don't get it. Ever been up to the big house, Dalton?"

Dalton sang another verse and tapped his fingers on the table.

"Hey!" The cop smacked him upside the head. "I'm talking to you, jackass. Who the hell do you think you are, singing when I'm speaking to you?"

There was a tap on the mirror, and the door opened. Into the interrogation room walked a woman in her thirties with blonde hair that almost touched her shoulders. Around her neck hung her name badge. But Dalton didn't need to read the name.

It was Jax. His heart beat pounded in his ears. He wanted to jump up and wrap his arms around her, explain everything. But people he did not know were watching.

This presented an entirely different set of problems. In a flash he realized that he had to act as though he did not know her. She did not say his name. Nor did she look at him directly. It was very difficult, but he knew people were watching, so he forced himself to not shift his stare from the wall for more than a second.

"Sergeant," said the woman, "if I ever see you strike a prisoner again, I don't care if your captain is standing behind that mirror. I will have your badge before the end of the day. Is that clear?"

The fat sergeant hoisted his belt and turned to the mirror. "Yes, ma'am."

"I'm taking over this interrogation."

He grumbled something and rounded up his paperwork, picked up his cup of coffee and threw it against the wall, and marched out of the room.

Jax took an entirely different approach. She sat on the edge of the table and shuffled through the paperwork. "I'm sorry about that officer. Can I get you anything to drink?"

He knew he had to maintain the interrogation strategy he had been using before she entered the room. Dalton didn't know who was behind the mirror observing their interaction, but he had to assume there was more than one high-ranking officer there.

He tapped his fingers on the table and sang a few lines.

"My name is Jax Taylor. I work for the district attorney's office. I've been sent to determine whether you're going to stand trial. However, it seems that you may possess knowledge of the whereabouts of certain artworks that are extremely valuable, and wanted in foreign countries. If you are willing to divulge this information, or help the authorities locate these artworks, there may be a deal I could work out for you."

Jax read a list of the charges. She went over and over the questions regarding the basement and the body that had been found, and whether or not the dead FBI agent had any connection with Dalton.

That was what she was supposed to do. Dalton, however, continued his game of staring at the wall, tapping his fingers.

At some point during the questioning, Jax raised her hand and brushed her cheek. On that hand she was wearing the ring Dalton had given her years before. Not only was she wearing it, but she must have been pushing it with her thumb, because the ring moved about on her finger. She only did it for a moment, when she was turned with her back to the mirror, and had positioned herself at the exact spot in the room where she would not be seen on camera.

It was a message. It had to be.

❊ ❊ ❊

Three hours later, Dalton was sitting in a holding cell. The electronic latch on his cell door sounded with a loud noise, and the door popped open an inch or two, and continued to slide open. He looked up to see two jailers. One of them held a clipboard with a bunch of papers. He sorted through the papers and called Dalton's name.

"Jason Dalton, you made bail. You're a free man."

"Who paid?"

Nick and Singh were waiting when he came through the metal door and walked out into the public area.

"How'd you pay the bail?" he asked.

"Don't look at me," said Nick, as they walked down the steps and out into the fresh air. "It was Singh."

"You bailed me out?"

Singh raised his hands into the air above his head. "Yes, because I am working with an American detective. It is so exciting. But I'm looking at the big picture here with Solomon's Key. Don't think it's because I want to sleep on your cold tile floor and make rice and curry in your ugly office. Okay?"

"Don't hold back, okay? Just say what you really think," said Dalton.

"What happened back there, boss?" asked Nick, but got no response as they walked out of the station.

They hurried around the block and walked to the parking garage. Somewhere a car alarm was going off.

"We have a couple of new twists to this case," said Dalton as they neared the car. "First of all, that Italian commander had two motives for coming into our office. Not only was he there to offer us a partnership, but he got my fingerprints. All he had to do was grab a pen or a paperweight. Then he had fingerprints to plant wherever he wanted. I thought I was turning the tables on him by getting his squad to go trample about on that crime scene where the body was. But it looks like he took out the competition by sticking one of my fingerprints beside the body."

They climbed into Singh's rental car. At the first light they came to, their way was blocked when the security barrier came down and allowed a trolley to pass.

"And what's the other twist?" said Nick.

"That one's a little harder to take. I think Sophie Devonshire has lawyered up. That means she has most likely been advised to distance herself from us. I suspect her attorney is trying to shift blame for the murder to yours truly, and portray her as the innocent, unaware landowner."

"And the artifact? How are we going to find it?" As always, Singh shook a hand in the air as he spoke.

Once they got back to the neighborhood, Singh slowed down and cruised along in the right-hand lane, searching for a parking spot.

"Why don't you let me out here?" Dalton rolled his window down and looked up and down the sidewalk.

"I'll go with you," said Nick.

"Did you bring my backup?" Dalton turned and looked into the backseat.

"Yeah, I have it." Nick leaned forward and reached under the seat and came up with a revolver wrapped in a white towel. "Are you sure this thing will even fire anymore?"

Dalton took the pistol, pressed the lever on the side that allowed the cylinder to drop open, and made sure it was loaded. With his thumb he spun the cylinders and flipped the weapon to one side so that the cylinder snapped into firing position. "It'll work. Don't worry about that. You guys need to go back to the office and do all the research you can about that artifact. If we find it, the Italians and Israelis will go away. Then I can concentrate on this bogus murder charge."

"Where are you going?"

"I'm going dark. You're not going to hear from me."

"What should I do with that suitcase if you don't come back?" asked Nick, shoving his hair back.

Dalton opened his door and climbed out. He leaned down close to Nick. "Well, pay back Singh, take care of Jax, too. Then, you're gunna pack it up into a backpack, and walk across the border. Maybe you can open your own detective agency somewhere." He clapped Nick on the shoulder, and hurried away.

CHAPTER 19

What do you say to your dream woman? Dalton didn't know. For two years he had kept a vision of Jax in his head. He had replayed the memories so many times that now he wondered if he had mixed fantasy with reality and created a perfect woman who had never really existed. If that was the case, he accepted it. He wanted to see her in that cheerleader outfit, needed to remember her lying beside him, gazing with loving eyes.

He went to those memories as he sat on the bench in Little India. Women walked along Artesia Boulevard wearing saris. Men wore business suits and sandals and called to children who ran about the sidewalk. Even out here in the open air, he could smell aromas drifting from restaurants along the street, restaurants that brought Indians to this area from as far away as Moor Park, Thousand Oaks, and Dana Point.

He was amazed to see that the little jewelry shop was still there. How many years ago was it that he had played hooky from school and come down this way with Ted? That day, they had seen a little window display. And on a small black felt tray that held a few other rings, sat the ring that was now on Jax's finger. The way she'd moved the ring in the interrogation room had to have been a message. Either it was a clever way to signal him, to send a message that no one else would pick up on, or she was scratching her finger, and that made the ring move about. He was going to find out in just a few minutes.

Moments later, Jax came walking down the street from the north, and paused in front of a window. Gone was the business suit she had been wearing, the pinstripe slacks and the stiff white shirt beneath the vest. Jax was always cold, that much he remembered. And even now, on a pleasant SoCal evening, when the temperature barely got below seventy, she wore tight Levi's and a big loose sweater that looked fuzzy even from across the street.

Dalton walked a big loop along the street and checked twenty times to make sure they were not followed. He headed over a block and then behind a couple restaurants, and there he turned back through the parking lot behind the jewelry store, and walked up the alley between a clothing store and a market. He made an effort to walk quietly, being careful where he placed each foot in the loose gravel, trying not to kick any rocks that would shoot up ahead of him and warn anybody out past the shadows, anyone up ahead on the sidewalk. When he came into the light, he slowed his pace until she looked over. Then he turned back into the passageway and walked into the parking lot.

"Dalton?" She gasped and covered her mouth with a hand.

He stepped toward her, but she raised her hand with a motion that said no, just stay there.

"Oh Dalton, why would you do that? You just left without any warning. You know how much that hurt?"

He raised his hands. "I tried to protect you. We had a computer breach. Two families were executed by the cartel. I couldn't let that happen to you."

Jax pulled her sleeves down over her hands and sobbed into the wool. "I never believed that funeral crap. I searched and searched for answers. I knew you were alive, you fucker." She ran at him and hit him several times with wild blows about his head and chest.

He stood there dazed, not knowing what to do, wondering if he deserved all this. And then he reached out and grabbed her and pulled her against him. He held on as she struggled and moaned and spit.

"I even hired someone to search for you, a career officer. I thought another army officer would be able to get the truth."

"Tell me it wasn't Major Thomas Trenton Gregory that you hired."

Jax stopped struggling and stepped away. "How did you know?"

"I think he shot Ted."

"Our Ted, from high school? Why would Gregory shoot Ted?"

"Maybe he got greedy. My researcher found that Gregory was running a sideline business, a gun for hire on the dark net. The short answer is money. If he knows about the Key or the blocks of cash, that's his motivation right there."

"Key? Blocks of cash? This doesn't sound good, Dalton. What are you involved in?"

"Where do you meet Gregory?"

"I asked what you were involved in." Jax crossed her arms over her chest and tilted her head to the side.

"I'm a private investigator, working on a case. Come on. Let's get out of here. I'll tell you all about it on the drive."

* * *

It wasn't the car Dalton expected. He imagined a late-model coupe, most likely at Toyota or a Nissan that would blend in on the freeway with a million other cars just like it in LA. But no, that wasn't Jax's style. She had to be different, and her car announced her difference to everyone. Dalton stopped when she put her key in the door of a 1971 MG convertible.

"You're joking, right?"

Jax laughed and tossed her hair over a shoulder. "You can always take the bus, if you prefer. In fact, I'd really enjoy seeing that."

"What is it with you and Ted? That's what he told me when I didn't want to get into that muscle head car of his."

The rear wheels spun and threw gravel as the MG shot out onto Artesia Boulevard and headed south through Cerritos and Hawaiian Gardens, where Jax drove onto the freeway.

As they drove, Dalton told her the whole story about Sophie Devonshire, the blocks of cash, and the dead body.

* * *

Jax pulled up behind the commercial building that Ted had shown him. She jerked the parking brake, jumped out of the car, unlocked the gate and pushed it open. Once they were inside, Dalton climbed out and rolled the gate shut.

The building was narrow and long, with a high ceiling. They entered through the back door and had to work their way along a path between moving boxes, around half-filled drawers and three racks of shoes. Jax went about the living room turning on lights and pulling blinds.

Dalton turned to say something, but Jax covered his mouth with a hand and stepped close, staring into his eyes. "Before you say a word, you need to sit."

Jax moved a couple of stacks of books from the sofa, and they sat.

She leaned forward, hands clasped between her knees, and stared at the floor. "I waited for you. Two years, and you didn't even send a note."

"Jax, would you do anything to save me?"

She didn't look at him. "You know I would."

"I had three minutes to decide whether I'd keep you by my side and risk losing you forever, or keep you safe by dying. One note could have meant your death. I couldn't even think about losing you. You're all there ever was for me."

She cried and only dared to glace toward him as she said, "Do you still want me?"

"You're all I ever wanted." He reached over and touched her leg with a slow, cautious movement.

She laughed through the sobs and jumped across the sofa and wrapped her arms around Dalton. "But you never leave. Whatever happens, we fight it together. Promise me now."

He laughed. "Yes, I promise." He tasted salty tears on her lips.

For a long time, they lay there whispering about the case, sharing bits of their lives.

When he got up and asked about the bathroom, she said, "Be careful in the back there. I have a contractor remodeling. His tools and supplies are everywhere."

When he returned, Dalton was holding a metal wire with a wooden handle at each end.

"What is that?" she asked.

"It's a garrote. Give Gregory a call. Tell him that I sent you a note about a block of cash. You need to meet him."

"Are you sure you want to confront him? He taught hand-to-hand on the base."

"Good. So did I. Gregory shot Ted. All I'm going to do is turn him. We might need an ace in the hole by the time this case is cleared up."

* * *

He'd have to wait, but hopefully not too long. Dalton knew Gregory's car. He'd seen it before. He'd also seen the huge Samoan driver. If he played this right, the driver would never know that Gregory was in trouble.

Dalton sat up on the roof behind a tree where the branches provided cover. He chose a spot and sat down where he could watch the entire street. A couple hours passed, and the air felt cold on his face and hands. He stretched his legs and rubbed his face to keep from dozing off.

The black Town Car turned onto the street and drove slowly along, quiet as could be. It stopped directly across from Jax's building, and the driver jumped out and walked around and opened the door for Major Gregory.

By the time Gregory stepped onto the sidewalk, Dalton had slid down the drain pipe on the side of the building. In darkness, he crept around the front.

The instant the major reached for the doorbell, Dalton slipped the garrote over his head and tightened it around his throat.

There is no mistaking that feeling of cold wire poised to cut off the breath of life. The major tried to shout, but the wire tightened. His arms shot up. He clawed at the wire, hopping about as though he could summon the force to resist strangulation. Then his brain caught up with the physical reaction, and he realized what had just happened.

"Answer my questions or I'm gunna cut your fucking head off and roll it down the street like a bowling ball. Do you understand me, Major?" Dalton gave the wire a tiny little jerk, and the man gagged.

"My right leg; that means yes. You tap my left leg; that means no. You understand?"

Gregory found Dalton's leg and thumped it with his hand.

He leaned close to the Major's ear and whispered: "Somebody paid you to get information about a certain artifact. Is that correct?"

He tapped Dalton's right leg.

The car door slammed. Dalton glanced over his shoulder to the Town Car. The Samoan driver was walking quickly toward him.

The driver peeled off his suit, threw his blazer onto the trunk lid, pulled his tie out of his collar, grabbed his shirt, and tore it open. The buttons popped off and fell into the street.

Dalton could've finished Gregory with a quick jerk, but he wanted information. He released the wire and ran onto the sidewalk to meet the running driver.

He had one shot. He knew that. This guy was huge and was coming at him like a truck. If the Samoan got a hold of him, he'd pull Dalton apart like an angry terrier ripping apart a doll.

The driver didn't even try to get into a fighting stance. He didn't raise his arms to shield his face or turn sideways to make his vital organs less of a target. Everything about the guy, from his massive shoulders to his barrel chest, to the demented smile, was saying, you got five seconds to live.

Dalton ran to meet the guy and threw all his force into a punch to the Samoan's solar plexus. It was a perfect blow that would've shattered the chest bone of most adversaries. But the Samoan hardly flinched.

The driver swung twice. Dalton dodged each punch easily and danced away. Speed was his greatest weapon now, and he hit the guy three times in the face, then jumped sideways and jabbed him in the kidney. The kidney blow stunned the driver.

He barked, and staggered forward.

That was when Dalton kicked him in the knee and knocked him to the ground. The guy fell with such force that the sidewalk shook.

Normally Dalton would've felt happy, and relieved that he had survived. But as soon as the driver hit the sidewalk, the Major swung a baton.

The black metal club didn't look like much. But Dalton had seen an MP snap a man's forearm with one. He jumped away from the first two swings and was moving with the rhythm of the Major's swings, waiting for his chance to jump in and put the guy down, when a massive hand clamped around his ankle like the jaws of a vise. It pulled him backward.

The Samoan driver might have been on the pavement, but he had not given up the fight.

Dalton struggled to remain standing. He thrust his arm up to block the baton and expected to hear the bone shatter.

A flash of movement entered his peripheral vision, and a shovel came down on Gregory's shoulder. The major cried out and dropped to his knees.

Jax gathered the shovel and drew it back to hit a home run on the guy's head, but Dalton stopped her.

"That's enough." He grabbed the shovel and pushed it aside.

The Samoan driver crawled forward on his elbows and looked up at his boss. "Major Gregory, I'm still good. You want him taken out?"

The major laughed and grabbed his shoulder as he wrenched about on the ground. "You hit me with a fucking shovel. I think you broke my shoulder. I thought I was working for you, Jax. What is wrong with you?"

"I thought you were working for me too. And then I was surprised by two military goons trying to oversee my questioning of Dalton. I knew right there that somebody had been leaking information about his whereabouts."

Dalton moaned and climbed to his feet. "Come on," he said, and tried to lift Major Gregory.

"Oh, not that shoulder."

Dalton walked to the other side of the major and helped him climb to his feet. "Come on, let's get you guys inside."

There was a lot of groaning and complaining as the four of them stepped inside the house. The moment they came through the door, Jax separated herself from the others, and found chairs for everyone.

"I didn't sell you out, Jax. I was ready to capture Mr. Dalton here, and turn him over, so I could collect my final paycheck. I had nothing to do with those guys showing up at the interrogation." Major Gregory stood up and sat back down as he tried to find a position that would make his shoulder feel better.

"Let me see your arm." Dalton stepped over and lifted the major's arm. "This is going to hurt for a second." Before he'd even stopped speaking, he twisted the arm and popped it back into the socket.

The major shouted and dropped onto the sofa. A second later, he lifted his arm and wiggled his fingers, a perplexed look on his face. "How did you do that? It feels so much better."

"I found a couple bugs on me a while back. Did you plant

them?"

Gregory shook his head. "No, that's not the way I work."

Dalton told him the whole story of the case, about the Key, the Israelis, and the man from the Vatican. He also mentioned a price he was going to pay Gregory for his service.

"I have another job that I need your help with. I assume you hired the two maniacs that came into my office with the beanbag weapons."

"That's correct. Freelancers."

"And you have access to those weapons?"

"I do, and many others."

"I'm going to stand this case on its head."

"What's in it for me?"

"How does fifty-thousand sound?"

"That's a good price for a short-term op."

"Six days max, that's all it should take. At the end of six days, I'll hand you fifty-thousand."

"You have my full attention. My driver and I are working for you."

"You don't touch Ted again."

"That was business."

When negotiations were finished, Jax led everyone to the door and shut it behind Gregory and the driver. She waited a minute, listening to their footsteps departing. Then she carefully locked it, spun the latch on two deadbolts, and turned.

"You can't trust him."

"I know. But I need those weapons."

Dalton lifted her off her feet and pushed her against the wall.

"Two years is a long time."

"Yeah. Let's go catch up."

CHAPTER 20

Dalton felt the cold air the moment he stepped out the door. It was that silent time in the city, between two and four AM, when most of the vehicles on the street were bakery trucks and newspaper delivery vans. A few workers were getting into their cars. He watched a guy leave his travel mug on the roof. Dalton hurried out into the street and grabbed the mug as the car pulled away. He just managed to tap the quarter panel before the driver was gone. The guy hit the brakes, gave the stranger a startled look in the side mirror, as though he was afraid Dalton was going to shoot him or something. Then he noticed the stainless-steel mug.

There was a commotion inside the car, and it backed up.

"I'm thinking you might need this." Dalton held out the mug.

"That would be the second one I've lost this month." The driver took the mug and laughed as he rolled up the window and drove away.

A few shops turned on their lights as he walked past. He hurried up the marble staircase and took his keys out as he approached the front door of his office. But the door, pieces of lumber screwed to it, was unlocked. Dalton put the keys back in his pocket, reached under his coat, and removed his weapon.

Music was playing. At least, that was what he thought it was, some techno music that the kids were listening to these days. Across the office, the tables had been pushed together. Every lamp was either standing beside a table or up on top, adding another source of illumination.

Two young men were talking gigabytes and megabytes and programs and algorithms. It was a language that Dalton did not speak. He slipped in, closed the door hard behind him. The two workers stopped typing and jerked upright.

Dalton aimed his gun and walked over. "Who are you?"

The smaller of the two men, who looked as though he hadn't entered puberty yet, stared at the weapon. "Oh, no, no no no," said the guy. He sat his energy drink down on the table and shook his hands in the air. "We're Nick's friends, from the computer club."

The other guy pushed off with his legs and rode his chair like a skateboard to the end of the table.

"Stop!" Dalton wagged the pistol. "You, move over here next to this guy."

The guy with the wheels on his chair jumped to his feet. "Mr. Dalton, we're working for you, sir!"

"Where's Nick?"

"He went to the airport. He took a flight to Fort Worth. We found something in the records that might blow this whole thing out of the water."

Dalton took a deep breath, walked to his desk as he pulled off his shoulder holster, and shoved the weapon into it. "So, what is going on?"

Out on the street, they heard someone shouting. Moments later a car alarm started going through its cycle of horns and siren noises. Two other car alarms began wailing. Dalton stepped to the window and looked down in the street below.

"Ted," he said, and waved to the computer guys. "Come with me."

The three of them ran down the stairs and helped Ted walk up to the office.

Once inside, Ted shouted, "Let go. I don't need little kids watching out for me." He walked over to Dalton. "Jax gave me a call and told me what was going on. You two are back together?"

Dalton nodded with long, slow movements of his head, and smiled from ear to ear.

"Will wonders never cease."

"What are you doing out of bed? They just took two bullets out of you."

"Shit. He shot me with a .32. What little boy carries a .32?" Ted groaned and leaned forward as his elbow pushed in against his side.

"I'm taking you back to the hospital."

"Like hell you are."

"You need to get better."

"I'm good. Where's that crazy Nick and your Indian guru, Singh?"

"Nick's in Texas, on the trail of something he thinks is gunna blow this case open."

"And Singh?"

"I don't know. He just wanders off."

Ted walked up close to Dalton and whispered, "Brother, if you got a plan to close this game out, then we need to do it. It's time to take our ball and go home, because these guys we're playing with are killers."

"I have a plan. But I need your help. Can you walk? Can you shoot?"

Ted stood up straight and smiled. "Just like high school, and old Ted's gunna keep them hoodlums off your ass. I got ya, brother."

The city had woken up by the time they got out of the building and down into the parking lot.

"I brought the Malibu. I thought it'd be faster than this Japanese rice burner you drive," said Ted.

Dalton opened his door and climbed into the car. He reached over and opened Ted's door. "It's not about how fast the car will go. Driving this car is about blending in. If someone sees a late-model foreign coupe, that means five out of ten cars on the freeway could be that car."

Ted held his side, groaned, and climbed in. "I got it. The Malibu would stick out like a sore thumb. Wherever we're going, I ain't going to be naked. What'd you bring for me?"

Dalton pulled out of the parking lot and pointed to the backseat by flipping a thumb over his shoulder. "Look under that blanket there. I got a couple of revolvers and a Glock."

Ted smiled. "See." He tapped Dalton's leg. "You brought something for me. If I had my ladies, we'd be set. But I knew my homie would take care of me."

"I need you to cover my back. Remember that basement in San Pedro I told you about? Well, something about it has been bugging me ever since I first stepped foot in there. I need to go back. There's something I'm not seeing. I just have this feeling that the Key is in there."

Ted reached between the seats and pulled aside the blanket. "That's an M1 carbine. Where have you been hiding this beauty?"

"There's a bag under your seat that has a couple of banana clips in it. Each one of those—"

"Each one holds thirty rounds. That's a lot of persuading."

They sat silent as Dalton cruised north on the 405, heading to the 110 that would take them straight down into San Pedro, and back to the basement.

"You feel better now?" Dalton said.

"I do. You know, I always want to be holding onto a little something with a trigger when I'm out and about with you, brother."

"I don't think we're going to have any trouble. Every police department in the world has been through that basement. So have the Italians and the Israelis. But I'll feel a lot better with you standing behind me with all that firepower."

"When this is all over and done, what do you think you and Jax are going to do? You gunna stop trying to save the world?"

"We've been talking about that. She has a good job with the DA. Maybe I'll continue being a PI."

"I wish you guys the best. Don't get your fingers caught in the gears of this case. Don't get caught in it."

"I hear you."

"Because I want to see your kids. Who else will teach them all the bad words for kindergarten?" He laughed.

"You'd do that for me?"

* * *

Dalton parked four blocks from the fountain house. After all the excitement of the FBI teams marching around with those big three letters in black and white on their backs, and television crews staking out the house, talking to the neighbors about what had happened, and what the police found, he knew the neighbors would be on edge. There wasn't any other way to get at the house, other than to simply walk up to it. They went one at a time: just pulled the yellow police tape up and hurried through the back gate. The house looked completely different inside after the FBI, then the local police, had searched through every book and paper, and dumped everything on the floor.

Dalton didn't feel good about being there. Approaching every doorway, he eased up to it, his chest pressed to the wall. Before he entered the next room, he poked his head forward, took a quick glance, backed up, and took another look. Then he stepped forward, his weapon pointing the way.

"What's got you so spooked?" Ted asked.

Dalton pressed his head against the wall looked up at the ceiling. It was covered with that rough acoustical coating that every contractor seemed to love in the 1970s. "I don't know. Been dreaming about this place. Can you make it down the ladder?"

"Yeah, I'm good."

Dalton climbed down into the basement and waited for Ted. He took the rifle from his friend and set it down, reached up and helped Ted step down into the darkness. He searched around for the light switch. Once he flipped it, everything changed. Every drawer from the desk had been thrown into a different part of the room. Papers lay strewn about the floor, and the bulletin board stood in a corner, broken in half. Spray-paint graffiti decorated two of the walls with ugly orange.

Ted pulled back the action on the M1 and pointed it in every direction that he looked. "Do whatever you have to do, but make it quick. I don't like this place, either. There's something spooky here."

"There's something I'm not seeing. I know it's here. A man like Devonshire is not going to take chances. He had a lot of time to find the perfect hiding place. He had money to make anything he wanted." Dalton put his hand on his chin, and walked slowly across the room.

"The only things you're going to find are trash and rats." Ted spun and pointed the gun at an unexpected sound. The noise had come from upstairs. He jerked the weapon against his cheek and aimed at the trap door.

"I remember how this room was, how it looked, before they tore it apart." Dalton walked over and lifted the chair off the floor so that it stood on its legs. After a moment he tilted it back as he had the first time in the basement, and looked under the chair. The key box was gone. He looked up at the massive iron-clad door that had once guarded the entrance into Devonshire's warehouse. The door stood open, calling to him. Dalton turned a circle, and remembered what he had told Nick: always look for what doesn't fit.

Footsteps sounded on the floorboards above. Dalton took out his weapon. Ted was already at the trap door with the M1 pressed against his cheek. He heard whispering and laughter.

"I think it's the graffiti artist back again. It's got to be kids."

"All right," said a young man in the room above. "I'll go first."

He got half-way down the ladder before Ted shoved the rifle into his back and said, "You got no business here, boy."

The teenager shouted and shot up the ladder and was half-way across the room by the time Dalton looked at Ted. "That means we got about five minutes before a black-and-white shows up. I'm guessing that kid runs straight to his parents and tells them that somebody is in the basement of the fountain house."

"What was I supposed to do?"

Dalton walked across the room to the ironclad door. He moved it on its hinges and listened to the creak. Then he flipped the light switch and looked inside the warehouse. The room was a jumble of furniture that had been toppled over and sliced open to make sure nothing was hidden inside the padding. Dalton pulled the door to close it, and noticed two scratches in the paint.

They could have been scratches from anything. Maybe workers had made them as they carried in the old tables, or the swords made in Damascus, or the steamer trunk that became a coffin. After all, they were just two scratches. That was when it hit him: two scratches, side by side.

Dalton reached out to touch the scratches, then looked at the chair across the basement, and ran over to it. That was what had been bothering him for so long. On the front of the chair were ornamental brass decorations that stuck out on each leg. They corresponded to the exact same height as the scratches on the door. He picked up the chair and rushed across the basement, and pushed it up against the metalclad door. The scratches lined up exactly to the brass decorations on the chair legs.

"Why would anybody be propping the chair up against an open door?"

"To hold it open. I do it all the time."

Dalton climbed on the chair and looked about the ceiling. "There's nothing, nothing I can see. Why would a rich guy shove this chair against this door if there wasn't a reason for it?" Before he'd even finished asking the question, Dalton turned and looked at the top of the door, the one section of the door that no one ever saw.

"That's it! Quick, give me a knife or a screwdriver. There's a hidden compartment up here."

CHAPTER 21

Ted kicked some things out of his way and moaned as he walked, poking about with his foot. "Okay, here you go, see if you can use this."

Dalton brushed off the top of the door and blew away the dust. He dug around with his fingers and pulled up a latch.

Ted poked him with the rifle. "What's up there? Is it Solomon's Key? Are we rich?"

"I don't know." Dalton dropped the screwdriver to the floor and jerked on the latch several times. A section of the door moved and pulled free. He reached inside and found something wrapped in cloth. He glanced at Ted as he unwrapped it and held it up to the light.

The flat silver object, about the size of a small pizza box, was covered with strange writing.

"That's it," said Dalton. "Solomon's Key. This is what everybody's killing for. How many people have spent their life searching for this thing?" He climbed down off the chair and hurried across the basement. Then he realized that he was walking way too fast for his friend, and hurried back and helped Ted up the ladder.

"What are we gunna do with it?"

"That's not up to me. I'll ask Mrs. Devonshire."

Once they got out of the basement, it took their eyes a few seconds to adjust to the bright light of the sun that was filtering in through the windows. The kids who had come to spray more graffiti on the walls were nowhere to be seen.

Dalton was bending over and reaching down to grab the trap door when a floorboard creaked and he looked up. Just past Ted, a man stepped through the kitchen doorway and smiled. There was no mistaking who it was. It was Uri Dent, the bald killer who had come into his office and executed two soldiers.

Just seeing Uri sent Dalton into that special place that soldiers go, where there is no sound, where movement slows, where the brain shifts out of rational thinking and takes the person into survival mode.

A split second later, Uri Dent showed why he was smiling. From his coat pocket he produced a hand grenade, reached over and pulled the pin, and tossed it across the floor as if he were bowling. There was no sticking around. As soon as he let go of that grenade, Uri jumped and ran back through the kitchen.

"Grenade!" Dalton grabbed Ted by the arm and pushed him into the trap door. There was no time for protests. Ted, the former linebacker, jumped into that hole and disappeared from sight. Dalton dove in after him.

He hit the ground, but it was soft. He realized that it was Ted that he'd landed on. That made him roll off to the side. He slipped in some papers, fell and hit his chin, jumped to his feet, grabbed his buddy, and pulled him to the warehouse.

"I'm bleeding!" shouted Ted, holding his side as he ran through the basement.

Dalton shoved him through the metal door and slammed it behind them, shoved his fingers into his ears. "Cover your—"

Ted already knew what was going to happen, and clasped his hands over his ears so the repercussion from the grenade would not blow out his eardrums.

Then came the blast. Dalton felt it blow its way underneath the door and rush past his feet. "Are you all right?" He reached over and grabbed Ted's arm.

"You landed on top of me. I'm bleeding pretty bad."

Dalton saw blood flowing between his Ted's fingers. "I have

to get you to the hospital."

He pushed open the door and walked out toward the trap door. Smoke was pouring down into the basement from the house. Through the trap door he saw flames.

"Were trapped," he said, pointing.

"Let's go back in the warehouse. Let the house burn down, and then we walk away."

"No! The whole building is going to collapse on top of us. We got to get up that ladder. I'd rather burn than die down here."

"I'm with you. Give me a push."

Dalton helped Ted climb up the ladder, and when he was halfway up he put his shoulder against Ted's ass and forced him up. He was sweating badly by the time they reached floor level. All Ted could do was flop out of the opening, onto his side.

"I can't go any further. I felt something tear in my gut."

"Bullshit. I ain't going without you. Give me your arm." He tried to pull Ted to his feet, and choked on the smoke that was billowing around them. A painting burst into flames and fell to the floor. It dropped forward onto the back of a chair. The flames from the painting climbed up the back of the chair.

"We can't make it through the kitchen." Dalton looked around and grabbed a lamp that was sitting on one of the tables, and yanked the cord from the outlet. He ran to the window and used the lamp like a fireman's axe, smashing the window from its frame, up and down the sides, knocking pieces of glass out onto the patio. As an afterthought, he tore down curtains and threw them across the room.

He ran back to Ted, grabbed him by the arm, and pulled him up. It was only eight feet to the window, and Dalton pulled him across the floor until they were in front of the opening.

He lifted with his legs, holding Ted around his armpits, and tried to get him to his feet. But Ted was too heavy. During the lifting, Dalton ended up sitting on the window ledge with Ted in his lap.

But that was the next best thing.

He leaned back and pulled Ted with him, and together they

fell right out the window, out of the house, away from the flames and the heat and the choking smoke; he landed on his back with Ted on top of him.

"Oh, damn," Ted coughed. He gasped for air as he climbed to his feet. "I can breathe again."

Dalton wrapped Ted's arm around his shoulders, and together they walked out past the fountain, and down the curved driveway to the sidewalk. They made it to the next house before Dalton looked over and saw that the neighbor's house was also in flames.

Ted moaned and grabbed his side and tried to hold the blood from spilling out. "Two houses burning? That doesn't make sense."

"Actually, it does. Those two houses were both owned by the Devonshire's. I think that second house also had a basement. At least that's what the guy at the county recorder said. It's my guess that's where Devonshire kept the records. I think that organization sent in Uri Dent to burn the loose ends."

"But records? The guy comes in with a hand grenade, and he's gunna burn records?" Ted was trying to make sense of it, but he was in bad shape. Making an effort to walk, he almost fell to the ground.

"You got to make it to the car, buddy."

"Who would send somebody to destroy records?"

"You said it yourself. Remember when I told you about those blocks of cash? You said that much cash always means trouble. Well, that much cash means there had to be a major organization. Now it's on the run. Word has gotten out that the boss is dead, and there could be a paper trail that leads straight back to the members of the organization. They're covering their tracks."

Ted raised his head. "Dalton, what if Sophie Devonshire knew all along what her husband was doing?"

Dalton repositioned his arms around Ted, and continued walking. "Then she's the one that sent the hand grenade. If that's true, we're screwed. You have to stop working those divorce cases."

Ted tried to laugh, but moaned. "I'm just saying."

"Just keep your mouth shut. Let me get you to the hospital."

"But we have the Key, right?"

"Yeah, I have it."

"We found the thing, so we get final payment, right?"

"Ted, shut up. You're about to die. Stop worrying about money."

When they got to the car, they climbed inside and Dalton took Solomon's Key out of his shirt and handed it to Ted. "Feel this thing."

"Whoa." Ted moved away. "I ain't touching that thing. You know how old that thing is? I mean, let's get real. That stinking thing was around before Jesus walked. There must be all kinds of crazy bad mojo going on with it. No brother in his right mind wants to touch it. You take it."

Dalton drove up to the first stop sign and looked right and left. "Are you kidding me? It's a piece of metal." He set it on the floorboard, and started to accelerate away from the stop.

But he'd noticed something. "Did you see that?" he asked, pointing to a parked car.

Ted looked over his shoulder. "What, that guy in the car?"

"That looked like Singh. What's he doing up here?" Dalton made a U-turn and pulled up behind the car. The driver was slipping down in the driver's seat, trying to hide.

He tapped on the side window. Singh looked up and climbed back into a regular sitting position and rolled down the window.

"Singh, what are you doing here? Are you following me?"

The Indian did that funny head bob thing, reached to the passenger seat, and picked up a sawed-off shotgun.

Dalton stepped out of the way. "What are you doing?"

Singh jerked the door handle and jumped to his feet.

"Yes, I am following you. Do you not think an Indian man can be a private investigator? You helped me before. Now I am here to help you."

Dalton grabbed the shotgun, flipped the lever, opened it up, and pulled out two shells, one from each barrel, and tossed them into Singh's car. "You listen here; I don't need your help."

Singh walked to Dalton's car, looked inside, shrieked with a loud voice, reached in and picked up the Key.

"My life is complete." He danced in the street, holding Solomon's Key, rubbing it as though he expected a genie to come out in a puff of smoke. "All my dreams have come true! All I wanted was to touch it and hold it and press it against my chest. Do you know what people would do to have this? Do you know how many people have died trying to find it, trying to protect it, trying to track it down? King Solomon himself held this in his hands."

Dalton grabbed it and climbed back inside his car. "Don't be following me. You're working with us, Mr. Singh. That means we tell each other what we're doing. I'm going to need your help with this, so stay close to the office. And don't mention to a single soul that I have this. If you do, people will die. Do you understand that?"

"Yes, I understand. I am not a fool like that skinny man you run around with who has the red hair. I am an educated man. And you listen here. I am happy to be working with you, to find a place for the Key. It is an honor."

"Do you want me to shoot his foot?" asked Ted. "That would make me happy. I'll shoot him and we'll drive away. We'll never have to listen to him scream or talk without shutting up." He took out his automatic and slid back the action.

"No, we can't shoot him. Nick has dibs. Singh just gets on people's nerves." Dalton started the car and backed away.

"If Nick was here, we could make Nick work with him. Then we wouldn't have to worry about either one."

Dalton chuckled and glanced sideways. "That's what I was thinking."

He pulled onto the freeway, and fifteen minutes later he pulled up to the hospital.

CHAPTER 22

Dalton pulled to the curb at the emergency room entrance, shoved the car into park, threw his door open and ran around to the passenger side. He grabbed Ted by the arm and started to pull him out, then saw the blood on the seat. It was dripping out the door onto his shoes, and that freaked him out. He pounded on top of the car and shouted to an ambulance crew; they were laughing as they carried a gurney down the stairs while looking at their cell phones.

"Hey," shouted Dalton. "Help me, I need help over here. I have a gunshot victim. I think he's bleeding out! He's going to die right here on the curb. Help me!"

The two EMTs looked at each other, shoved their cell phones into their pockets, and went into emergency mode. One of them grabbed the front of the gurney, while the other went to the rear, and together they ran down the steps and swung the gurney over the curb and into the gutter as it rattled on the asphalt. The instant they got to the passenger door, they pulled Dalton out of the way. In an instant they had Ted up on the gurney and strapped in, and were running back toward the emergency door exit, shouting at people to get out of their way as they came barreling up the steps.

When they got into the waiting room, one of them ran to the glass window where a young nurse was chatting with an associate. The EMT shouted through the opening, reached in, and slapped an emergency button. An alarm rang somewhere down the hall. Within seconds a young doctor burst through the doors and met the gurney.

Dalton heard the word "gunshot" thrown around as the doctor sliced open Ted's shirt with a pair of scissors, pulled off the bandage and looked at the wound.

"Where was he treated before?"

Ted answered with a weak voice.

Dalton came into the emergency examining room and leaned over Ted.

"I need you to leave now!" said the doctor.

"You know what you have to do, right?" asked Ted.

Dalton leaned forward and whispered, "I'm going to find that fucker who threw the grenade."

"You need to get to that woman, the client, and find out what's going on. And you need to get paid."

"Okay, Ted. They're going to take care of you now. If you get a package, don't let anyone look inside." He winked.

"Brother, just finish the case and be there for Jax. She never gave up looking for you. I saw how she fought." Ted closed his eyes and flinched.

Dalton walked through the two big doors and stepped out into the hall. At nearly every door stood two or three people. A doctor in a white lab coat stood before a small group. He walked slowly down the hall and out into the waiting room with the different colored tiles forming patterns on the floor. On the tiles stood stiff, hard chairs that could not be moved. He sat down and thought over his options. All of a sudden, he was alone. Nick had taken a flight to Texas to find some hidden records about the Devonshires. And now Ted was in a hospital bed, unable to move.

Dalton wanted to feel sorry for himself. He felt numb. He wanted to lie down and sleep, just forget about everything. But his training wouldn't let him do that. And his training was shouting about the two men marching toward him.

It was their walk that alerted him. Here in this hospital,

where every visitor forgot about themselves and looked sad and concerned for loved ones, these two were walking toward him in military fashion, shoulder to shoulder, heads held high, strutting a bit. Even though they were dressed in T-shirts and jeans, one with a hood pulled over his head, there was no hiding the military swagger.

Dalton thought about the Key. Was it still in the car? It must be, he knew, or these two goons wouldn't be coming for him. There was no use in playing games. He knew what they wanted, and they knew that he knew. He saw the smile of acknowledgment cross their faces when they were fifty feet away.

Out of one of the rooms came a member of the hospital staff, a heavy black woman pushing an IV stand. Dalton grabbed the stand, twisted the little lock that allowed it to become taller or shorter, and separated the two halves. It was such a fluid movement, him stepping aside, grabbing the stand, spinning and swinging right into the approaching man, that it caught the two soldiers off guard.

He hit the first one across the forearm. Dalton followed his swing by stomping on man's foot.

The soldier grunted and fell backward and crashed against the wall.

The second man grabbed the IV stand before Dalton could swing it again. That meant that both the guy's hands were out of position, leaving his entire midsection vulnerable to attack.

The instant Dalton released the stand, he brought his elbow down and broke the second guy's collarbone. His other arm came at the guy with a wide swing and connected with the man's ear.

Somewhere in the corridor a woman screamed, and men shouted. There were loud voices behind him as Dalton pushed open the doors and hurried across the lobby, and rushed into the fresh air.

He didn't know whether to laugh or to be angry when he saw Singh sitting behind the steering wheel of his car.

"Hey, what are you doing?" called Dalton, as he ran down the steps. "What are you doing in my car?"

"What am I doing? You left the Key, Solomon's Key, lying there on the floorboard of your car like it was a toy for anyone to come along and take it and be gone into the night so that we could never find it again. Oh, my God. You call yourself a detective, but you leave this museum piece, this jewel of history, a map to the greatest wealth that the world has ever seen, just lying in your car like a discarded junk-food wrapper." Singh opened the door and jumped out of the car.

Dalton put his hand on the man's shoulder. "I know, Singh. I was thinking about Ted."

"I saw the blood, Mr. Dalton. I am very sorry about your friend. There were also two very large men that I saw enter the hospital. They did not look like nice people. I thought they were the associates of the men who were chasing us that day on Signal Hill. I had the hardest time finding this hospital, but I knew that you would return to home ground when you were in trouble, so I googled hospitals around Long Beach, and that is how I found you. And then I saw those two men, and I knew I had to put myself in your car so that they would not come snooping around there."

"Yeah, you did good." Dalton stepped around him and slid into his car.

Singh climbed into the shotgun seat. He repositioned himself about twenty times as he tried to avoid touching the blood.

"You still have it, right?"

"Certainly, yes, I have it." Singh reached under his seat and pulled out Solomon's key, and brushed it off with his hand. Even after it was clean he continued to rub it.

Dalton pulled away from the curb, and turned out onto Atlantic Avenue, and headed up toward the freeway.

"You were all alone with it, Singh. What kept you from running away and posting your findings in some academic journal and making yourself a hero?"

Singh sucked in air as though he had been underwater for a long time without being able to breathe. "Because I am a good man. How could any man hope to profit from something that is not rightfully his own?"

Dalton turned and looked at him long enough to see whether he was pulling his leg. "That's what I was thinking. I don't know who to give this thing to. I'm going to need your help. Do you still have that shotgun?"

Singh clapped his hands together and hopped up off his seat a couple of times. "Oh yes, I do, and I would really enjoy being able to shoot it one or two times at one of those bad brutes."

"Bad brutes," whispered Dalton, and laughed. "Okay, I have a little plan to end this thing. But Nick is gone, and Ted is not available."

"We will finish up this nasty business with these nasty men, and when it is finished we'll take Solomon's key to a nice clean academic museum, and turn it over to the proper authorities who will know exactly what should be done with it. That way it will be out of our hands, and into the history books it will be written."

"Is that what we should do with it, Singh?"

"Well, I believe that would be the proper procedure." Singh turned from Dalton and stared at passing cars.

"Even if the owner of the key does not want it, even if the owner refuses to take it because it might incriminate her in her husband's wrongdoings?"

※ ※ ※

The courthouse was busy. Lawyers with white shirts and ties that constricted their necks, rushed up and down the steps, their shiny black shoes tapping the concrete. Some carried briefcases. Others climbed the steps with stacks of files at their chests, leather satchels or briefcases in their other hand as they ran, trying to make it to court on time. Beside many of the attorneys rushed their clients. Some of the clients were dressed in jeans and work boots, and T-shirts with the names of rock bands.

Dalton led Mr. Singh up the stairs and into the third-floor corridor, and walked from courtroom to courtroom, reading the small plaques beside the doors that identified the trial about to take place. When he found the one he wanted, they moved away about twenty feet and stood with their backs against the wall, waiting and watching.

"That's her," said Dalton, gesturing by lifting his chin in the direction of the courtroom. "All you have to do is get close to her and whisper: 'I believe it's the rainy season in Honduras.' As soon as you say that, turn and walk out of the courtroom, and hurry down the corridor and down the stairs, where I'll meet you."

Singh did that funny wobbling thing with his head. As he walked away, he repeated what he'd been told to say.

Dalton waited out on the steps and watched attorneys and clients. In the distance a food truck was set up in the patio area between the office buildings. Around it, people stood at concrete tables. Off to the side, a group of skateboarders were hopping their boards up onto a concrete planter. They rolled along for a few feet, dropped onto the walkway, and shouted at friends.

Singh hurried through the doors and took his place beside Dalton.

A moment later, Jax burst through the door, paused for a moment, and acted as though she was stretching as she repeated the phrase about the rain in Honduras. She hurried down the steps and walked toward the food truck.

He followed her past the truck, past the diners, and around the corner of a parking structure. There he stopped and looked around to see which way she had gone.

"Where is she, Singh?"

But he didn't wait for an answer as he hurried into the parking structure. The instant he entered the shade of the structure, somebody grabbed him from behind and spun him around and jumped into his arms and shoved him against the wall, kissing him with breathless passion.

"Mr. Dalton, you're a fugitive, a dangerous man. I can't be

seen with you. I may have to run away and contact the authorities about your whereabouts."

"I'm trying to get some attorney-client privileges." Dalton kissed her.

"Oh, this must be the young woman from last night." Singh came through the doorway.

"You were following me last night?" asked Dalton, pushing Jax away.

Singh turned around like he didn't know which way to go or look, and hunched his shoulders. "I was protecting you, my friend. I sat outside this woman's house all night, on that terrible street in Los Angeles, only me and my little shotgun, trying to protect you, waiting for bad men to come."

"I almost got killed there. What happened to you?"

"Oh. I am so sorry. I fell asleep. But if I had seen anything, I would have come running."

"My name is Jax," she said, coughed, and brushed her hair out of her face as she extended her hand.

"I'm sorry," said Dalton. "This is Dr. Singh, the guy that could have rescued us last night. He's the guy that identified Solomon's Key."

"It is a great pleasure and an honor to meet you, Ms. Jax."

She shook his hand and looked at Dalton, as though waiting for more explanation about why this Indian man was with them. But when the explanation didn't come, the investigator in her went on without help.

"And why were you following Dalton?"

"All my life I have been studying to advance my position in life. My entire childhood was spent reading books and studying to take tests and speaking in classrooms surrounded by others who were trying to do better than I was. That continued right into my professional life. By the time I looked around, I was forty-five years old and still sitting at a desk and studying books and reading and writing books so that other people could read them while they were studying and spending their life with written words instead of going out and living life."

"The point is, he wants to make sure the Key gets to a good museum, and is not taken by bad people. Right?"

"Yes."

"Oh, and I forgot to tell you: Once he starts talking, he'll never shut up," said Dalton.

"And then one day this Dalton and his crazy redheaded friend burst into my life like cowboys shooting it out in the Wild West. We went for a crazy ride and drove right over the side of a cliff in an ugly little Volkswagen. It was so exciting! My blood was racing, my heart pounding, and fear was grabbing me with all its might." Singh's eyes grew large and he stomped on the ground as he spoke.

Jax stepped away.

"And that was when I realized that I wanted to live. I was involved in something that could shape history. I wanted to be part of it instead of reading about it. I wanted to shape it. I held in my hand Solomon's Key. This artifact that people had fought for and died for and dreamed about, this thing of legend that small children hear about and dream about before they fall to sleep at night. We have Solomon's Key. And I chose to be here, to put my books aside, so that I could watch over it and keep it safe and make sure that it gets into the right hands. And let me tell you, it has been so exciting." Singh stopped and wiped spittle from his cheeks, and looked around.

"Don't worry; he's always like that."

Jax backed away a bit farther. "Well, Mr. Singh, I'm glad to have you along. I know Dalton here is a good man. I'm very happy that you're watching out for him. Why don't both of you come back to my car? I need to tell you what's going on with this case."

"My car," said Dalton. "Three of us won't fit in yours."

They hurried out of the garage and walked past the people at the concrete tables and those grouped around the taco truck ordering food, some standing back, trying to read the menu, trying to decide what they were going to have.

Once they were inside Dalton's car, Jax began.

"Listen, I have to make this quick. I'm late for court and have to get back. But what you have to know is that Devonshire's lawyer is moving fast. She's already been deposed. They're making a case against you, Dalton. Her lawyer is claiming that you broke into the basement on your own, and that she had no knowledge of you prior to that. A murder took place on her property, so her lawyers are trying to distance her from that action."

"I didn't kill anyone. Hell, whoever that was in the trunk got killed several months before I was there. That level of decomposition doesn't occur overnight."

"I know you didn't do it. Between us, that's not in question. But what you have to remember is that this is going to be a court of law. We have to be able to prove you did not do it."

"That explains how Devonshire's organization was able to get the paintings and other artifacts into the country. The dead guy was probably going to get paid by Devonshire with the cash we found, but something went wrong. Maybe he got greedy and asked for more money, and Devonshire or one of his henchmen killed him."

Jax reached over and took hold of Dalton's arm. "The killing of a federal agent is not taken lightly by the feds. They are all over this case, and they're looking for someone to hang it on. If you have evidence showing that Sophie Devonshire contacted you about going into that basement, or investigating her husband, or anything showing that she had a contract with you to investigate anything in her life, then you need to get that evidence to your lawyer."

Dalton tapped his head against the headrest several times. "I can't believe she's hanging me out to dry like that."

"Look, you can't take this personally. It's gone legal. As soon as she turned it over to her lawyer, it was out of her hands. She's fighting for her life. You're fighting for your life. If you have evidence showing that she had a contract with you, Dalton, that's the only thing that might keep you out of prison. I don't want to lose you again."

"I have evidence. I have a digital recording of her coming into my office the same day a crazy man came and killed two soldiers. I have her on camera handing me an envelope full of cash."

"That's it! She handed you an envelope full of cash? And you said you found a large amount of cash in the basement, right?"

"Yes."

"Have you checked to see if those serial numbers are close to the ones found near the dead body?"

"No, but I will."

"You need to get back and check. Then you need to get that video to your attorney."

"I can check the numbers, but Nick has the recording, and he's disappeared in Texas somewhere."

Jax leaned over and kissed him hard on the lips, then backed away. With her hand around the back of his neck, she shook him about. "Dalton, you have to promise me you're going to get out ahead of this. I spent the last two years trying to find your ass, and I don't want to visit you in a federal lockup. That ain't gunna happen."

Dalton looked over his shoulder to Singh. "I think it's time we got rid of the Key. Once that thing is with the proper authorities, I won't have to worry about the Israelis or the Vatican soldiers."

"A map that leads to a large treasure? Have you considered who we should turn it over to? If it goes to the Vatican, and they acquire the treasure, with that wealth they could gobble up five or six banks and become a major power."

"Maybe we should just put it on eBay and sell it to the highest bidder."

CHAPTER 23

"I think I know the best thing to do with the Key. Singh, you said your brother-in-law had a jewelry shop in Little India, right?"

"Yes, yes, a very good shop. He makes all his own pieces. If you need a ring for your young woman, I will be happy to get you a wonderful discount."

"Can he make a copy of the Key, just for show?"

Mr. Singh's mouth fell open. "Oh, Mr. Dalton is being tricky. You are planning something sneaky with the Key. I just know it. Why else would a private investigator need a copy of a priceless relic?"

"It has to be perfect, Singh. Perfect weight, color, everything. Can your brother-in-law's shop do that quickly?"

"Ha, yes. With nothing more than a photo he can copy the Queen's necklace. I'm not saying he makes copies of jewelry often, but he can do it, if there is a good fee involved."

"It has to be quick, and be able to fool an expert for a few moments."

"What are you planning?"

"We can't control what any museum does with the treasure, if they find it. Right?"

"No sir."

"I think that the Key needs to disappear. But the only way I can get the treasure hunters off my back is by having them search somewhere else."

"I see. How can a normal-looking man like you be so devious? I think I know what you are planning. If those bad men see the Key is not authentic, they will murder you with no second thought."

"Can you help me?"

"I am calling the jeweler now."

Traffic was moving along at forty miles per hour, and that was a miracle for an LA freeway. It moved at that speed just long enough for drivers to get their hopes up. Here and there it slowed down to almost a dead stop, before it picked back up.

They came into the Little India off the 91 freeway, and cruised along Artesia Boulevard. About a block from the restaurant area, where several of the Indian restaurants sat beside sari shops and markets filled with spices, they passed the jewelry shop.

"Make a right turn at the traffic light. I'm sure he will give you a very good price, and the quality is the best you can find anywhere." Singh opened his door when they arrived in the parking lot, climbed over the seat, and pulled a backpack off the floorboard; he shoved the Key inside.

Dalton grabbed his arm. "This has to be done in secret. Nobody finds out, do you understand?"

Singh leaned back against the car and tapped his forehead. "I didn't want to tell you this. But most of his business is making copies of expensive pieces for insurance companies." He glanced over his shoulder. "And he makes some for dubious people who might want to substitute a fake for a valuable piece, so it appears as if the real piece has been stolen. And that you did not hear from me. I said nothing."

"Okay," said Dalton, nodding. "I feel better." He shoved a stack of bills from the basement into Singh's hand.

"My commission," said Singh, pulling out two one hundred-dollar bills, and shoving them in his pocket. "Now, Mr. Dalton, I brought you here because this is the best place to have that copy made. You will see. The Indian underground will take care of you."

He watched Singh walk around the corner and disappear. Dalton was climbing into the car when his phone rang. He answered, and heard Nick's voice.

"Boss, I'm on my way back. You're not gunna believe this. I have information that will blow this case out of the water. I can't speak about it on the phone. Get to a computer and contact me. Remember how I told you to contact me?"

"Give me thirty minutes."

* * *

When Nick's image came on the computer screen in the library, Dalton thought it was the wrong person for a moment. Even Singh laughed because Nick was wearing a cowboy hat.

"Hey," said Nick. "When you need to get information in Texas, you'd be surprised what a cowboy hat will do. You should see my boots."

"Another time. What did you find?"

"When the team and I were digging into the records, I found a gap in Sophie Devonshire's life. For two years there was no written trail, no medical receipts or DMV records. It was as though she just vanished for those years. That made super detective Nick suspicious."

"Your point, Nick. What did you find?"

"Do I get a drum roll?"

"I'm gunna drum roll on your head."

"Okay, boss. Sophie Devonshire died in 2005. Our client is an imposter."

"She died?" Singh pressed his hands to his ears and dropped into his seat.

"You're sure about that? You have the death certificate? Witness reports? Please tell me there's a death certificate that will hold up in court."

"Yeah, boss. I got all the paperwork, and I had it notarized as well."

Dalton let out a big sigh and looked around the library. "If she died, who is the woman that hired us?"

Nick pulled his hat off and tucked his hair back. He flopped his hat back into place, cocked it up in the front like he was all full of himself on a Friday night, and approaching a good-looking woman in a bar. "Well, that's the ten-million-dollar question. I've been interviewing neighbors and teachers at the high school, and a few family members. Sophie and another girl, Sadie Crawford, were joined at the hip for years. They went everywhere together. When Sophie was hit by a hit-and-run driver, Sadie dropped out of school and moved away within a year of the accident."

"Our imposter's name is Sadie Crawford. Now that she's lawyered up, a DNA test is out of the question."

"We may not need that. Two neighbors and a teacher from school mentioned that Sadie had a large birthmark on her left forearm."

Dalton thought back to the afternoon he had gone to visit Sophie Devonshire in her office. He remembered the slender, beautiful woman, handing him a drink. He remembered her outstretched arm and how he had looked at it and wondered if she'd burned herself. "You did well, Nick. Get back to California. I need you here yesterday. We're going to put an end to this thing. Make sure you bring those documents."

❊ ❊ ❊

He headed to the car and drove in silence through downtown Long Beach. On Sixth Street he approached the Arts District. Over the top of one of the large craftsman homes that had stood there since the early 1900s, he saw his office building. Along the sidewalk ran a boy of about eight, chasing after his friend on a laser skateboard. A couple of elderly men were sitting on a lawn, watching the world go by. Everything looked normal.

He was about to explain to Singh why they were back at the office, when a black, unmarked car came screeching around the corner and blocked the street. Lights flashed in its grill. Dalton checked the rearview and watched a white SUV lock up its brakes and block the street behind him.

"Oh!" cried Singh. "My shotgun is in the boot. Let me get my shotgun." Singh climbed over the seat and into the back of the car, where he grabbed the top of the back-seat, jerked and pulled, trying to tear into the trunk.

"Leave it alone, Singh. We're not going to shoot it out with these guys." Dalton put both hands on the steering wheel. "Just keep your mouth shut if they ask you any questions. The only thing I want you to say is: 'lawyer.'"

The amplified voice shot down the street over a loudspeaker.

The two boys who were chasing each other, stopped in mid-stride. The old men stood up and walked to their porch, pulling their chairs behind them. Several people came out their front doors, looked about, and slipped back inside their houses.

It was the FBI. Dalton had been expecting them. Jax had warned him they were coming. They had lost one of their own and were kicking over every rock in the case, trying to find who had executed their agent. Men and women jumped from vehicles, and came toward Dalton with their weapons drawn.

"I'm a private investigator!" shouted Dalton out the window. "I'm carrying a concealed weapon, and I have a permit to carry it. I'm now exiting the vehicle."

It didn't take the agents long to lock him in handcuffs and take his weapon. Beside the SUV they surrounded him.

"Well if it isn't Lowenthal, the big slug. I heard you got relieved of duty."

"This is Jason Dalton. Dalton, this is senior agent Trent."

"We met," snapped Dalton. "You two look like Laurel and Hardy."

One of the agents laughed, then cut it short with a hand over his mouth.

Trent pushed to the front of the line and snatched the file out of Lowenthal's hand. The chewing gum in his mouth snapped as he flipped through the file. Across the back of his hand was a Marine Corps tattoo.

"You're an Army guy." Trent looked up and slapped the file shut. The gum snapped. "I was in the Marine Corps. Army is almost like being in the military, isn't it?"

"Ask the two jar-heads I left at the hospital. Do you always wait until the handcuffs go on before you antagonize your prisoners?"

"I have your fingerprints on a chest that contained the remains of an FBI agent."

"That's old news. Did you really have to come in with your siren screaming just to tell me what I already know?"

An agent at Dalton's car shouted, "The key does not fit the lock!" He raised a crowbar. "Do you want me to open the trunk?"

"The only way you're getting in that trunk is with a warrant," said Dalton.

"The car is clean," shouted a female agent, stepping away from the vehicle and closing the door.

"Okay." Agent Trent rubbed his hands together. "Take off the cuffs. The suspect is not going anywhere."

The agent behind Dalton removed the handcuffs.

"This should interest you, Dalton." Trent took out a photograph and held it up. It turns out this woman works for the district attorney. Her name—"

Dalton broke the guy's jaw with a right, then hit him again as he was dropping forward. He spun and danced backward, and hit another agent squarely on the forehead. A third agent, a woman, came at him with a baton. Dalton shoved her aside, and three agents wrestled him to the ground. "That's assault on a federal officer."

Lowenthal tried to bend over and help his boss stand up, but his belly prevented him.

"You piece-of-shit FBI. You're exposing a federally protected witness. That woman is going to be killed because of you. You had a corrupt agent. Now you're trying to cover it up. What happened to doing the right thing?"

In spite of his protests, agents carried Dalton to the nearest vehicle, shoved him into the backseat, and slammed the door.

From his seat, Dalton got a good view of Singh going ballistic. The Indian started jumping around and throwing his arms in the air and shouting. "Everyone on the street! You know Jason Dalton. You know he lives here with you in that office up there in that building. These police officers threatened his family. A member of his family is going to be killed just so they can make their case. Turn on your cell phones. Did you film what just happened? Everyone in these houses around me, call your police department. Tell them what happened. Put it on YouTube. Call the radio stations. Call the newspapers. Tell them the FBI is dirty! They had a member of their own department helping an illegal organization, and now they're trying to frame a hard-working citizen so they do not look bad."

Several agents shouted at Singh. When that had no effect, one of them wrapped him up in a bear hug and tried to pull him to the vehicle where Dalton was sitting.

"We see what you're doing!" shouted a bystander, shaking a chain-link fence.

A woman held up her cell phone. "That's right, we see who you are. We have your license plates. We have the whole scene on film. The ghetto has eyes, motherfucker." She turned and ran into her house, and locked the metal security door.

One of the black boys that went to Dalton's class, ran out onto the sidewalk and threw a rock that hit the car Dalton was sitting in. "That one there with the short hair, he showed a photo to Dalton. Ha! And my teacher, an army guy, he busted you right upside your ugly-ass head. Whooped your ass in public, a bad ass-whooping too." The ten-year-old boy laughed and ran up the block.

Singh ran over to Dalton and tapped on his window.

"Get to my office, Singh," Dalton instructed him. "Pull out the middle drawer of my desk and turn it over. On the bottom is a phone number. Call that number and tell the man what happened. Tell him my name. Don't forget, Singh. You do it, and you do it now. Go!"

* * *

They took him to the same facility he'd been in with Nick. Before this trip, he'd never suspected the building had a basement. Two large agents took him down in the elevator. Each held an arm as they escorted him past the line of cells. They opened one, pushed him inside, and shut the door. As they walked away, they joked about Agent Trent's broken jaw.

The cell was empty except for a toilet bucket in the corner. He chose a spot on the floor as far away from the bucket as he could get, leaned against the bars, and stretched his legs. He sat there for two hours before the same two agents opened his cell and lifted him to a standing position. Without a word, they led him to the elevator and into the light of day.

In a large, stark office, they shoved him into a chair and stood guard, one on either side. Behind a large desk stood a man with his back to Dalton.

"Sometimes I like to just stand here and look out past the parking lot, out toward the foothills in the distance. That would be Pasadena out that direction." The man turned from the window.

His chest and shoulders said he kept himself in shape. The top of his head was bald. The remaining hair around the sides was black and short. A tiny dot of blood on one cheek showed that he had recently shaved.

"I hear my agent was trying to play hardball, Mr. Dalton."

Dalton rubbed his wrists where the handcuffs had been, and looked at the man behind the desk. "What do we have when law enforcement officers threaten a person's family?"

The middle-aged man put his hands on his hips. "You have

an agent trying to extract information."

"Am I being recorded, sir?"

"No, Mr. Dalton. This conversation never took place."

Dalton nodded. "That's twice your agents have threatened to expose my fiancée. A lot of people went to a lot of trouble to protect my identity, and any connection I may have with that woman."

"Yes, I believe you. In fact, I just got a call from the director of the Bureau. Special Agent Trent is going to be eating through a straw for about six weeks. I'm sure he'd like to make you disappear in facilities that aren't supposed to exist. That would make me happy too."

"I have not been read my Miranda rights. I have not been charged with a crime. Nor am I here voluntarily. You are holding an American citizen against his will, without charging him with a crime."

"I've been told to give you up. It seems a certain officer whose name doesn't exist except in whispers among politicians, has taken a liking to you. In fact, I've been ordered to turn you over."

Dalton stood up. "It sure has been fun." He turned to leave, and looked out through the window that the man behind the desk had been preoccupied with. Out across the concrete, several vehicles were parked in rows. The entrance to the parking lot was a long chain-link gate, controlled by a booth.

Three Army Humvees were turning off the street and into the driveway. Even from the office, Dalton could hear the man in the lead Humvee shouting orders at the agent in the booth. When the gate did not open immediately, the lead Humvee crashed right through the gate and knocked it to the ground, dragging it halfway across the parking lot, where it smashed into a couple of parked cars and fell to the ground. The other two vehicles followed the first into the lot. The instant they stopped, six men in military gear ran toward the facility, shouting as they went.

The man in charge jumped to the pavement and shouted orders. He was tall, with broad shoulders and skin black as roasted coffee. From the floorboard of the vehicle, he picked up a loudspeaker. "You are harboring an officer of the US army. Deliver him now, or we will take him with extreme prejudice. You have thirty seconds."

Men and women ran down the hall and shouted orders. Dalton heard weapons being taken out of storage racks and loaded.

The man behind the desk pushed Dalton out of the way and stepped into the corridor. "All agents are ordered to stand down. If one weapon is discharged, that agent will be suspended indefinitely without pay. Do I make myself clear?"

Dalton was escorted out the back door and across the parking lot, where he was handed over to the military commander. He tried to keep the smile off his face as he climbed into the Humvee.

As the vehicle started to roll forward, the commander shouted to the driver: "Sergeant, take out that fence." He pointed.

"Sir, yes sir." The young driver pulled the wheel, and the vehicle swerved from the driveway and crashed through the chain-link fence, pulling most of it into the street before it broke free of the vehicle's bumper, and shot back toward the driveway like a broken rubber band.

The Humvee bounced over the road. Dalton held on tight to the bars that held the antenna above him. He thought back to the good old days, when half his life was spent in vehicles like this. But now it seemed strange to be sitting there in civilian clothes, without a helmet strapped to his head and an assault rifle in his lap.

"Major Dalton."

"Yes, Colonel."

"You are a pain in my black ass. You always have been. Do you know how many orders I had to disobey, how many favors I had to call in, just to get me out here today and rescue your butt?"

Dalton tried not to smile. "You got the call."

"Hell, yes. I take it your cover is blown."

"Like a claymore mine, Sir. The FBI threatened to expose my woman."

"You did the smart thing. The cartels never forget. It was your testimony that put what, ten of them in prison? That case got the DOJ a couple of feathers in their cap. And by 'cap,' I mean budget. We worked hard to get you this identity. I think we can make you disappear one more time. But no more after that."

"Thank you, sir. How's your son?"

"He's ready to graduate from university. That leg of his is doing just fine because you carried him out of that jungle hot zone."

"He was just a soldier under my command, Sir."

"You're just a soldier under my command, Dalton. You're staying at the Ritz Carlton tonight, and the Army is footing the bill, whether they like it or not."

"Are you feeling guilty for recommending me to Sophie Devonshire?"

"She told you?"

"Yes."

"I just wiped that debt clean."

"Hell yes!"

CHAPTER 24

Dalton rolled over, fluffed up the down pillow, and dropped his head onto it. He stretched a couple of times beneath the satin sheet, and wondered why the army never had beds like this when he was active. That moment of relaxation vanished quickly.

It was still an old habit that he'd developed during boot camp, the way he jumped out of bed and slapped his pillow flat, ironed out the wrinkles with his hand, and placed it perfectly back into position and straightened the covers. But he had to stop himself when he lifted the mattress and tucked the comforter between it and the box springs. This was not boot camp.

He was about to step into the shower when he heard a knock on the front door. Dalton jumped and searched the room for his 9-mm. At the dresser, he lifted his weapon and carefully pulled back the action to make sure that it was ready to fire. He walked in bare feet to the door.

Dalton squinted and looked through the spy glass. All he saw was an empty corridor and the room across the hall.

"What is it?" he called, pressing his back to the wall, breathing onto the barrel.

"It is eleven minutes past seven in the morning. I have been waiting in this hall for thirty-five minutes. It is time for you to get up. We need to get going, Mr. Dalton. It is going to be a busy day for you. Now, please open this door for your friend Singh, so that we can prepare everything that needs to be done to get rid of this nasty thing that has come into our lives."

Dalton opened the door. "I knew it was you the moment you opened your mouth. Nobody speaks like you, Singh."

"That is because I am so intelligent."

"Right." Dalton picked up the telephone and flipped through the menu that was laying on the side table. He ordered a large breakfast and hung up the phone.

"I got a call from Ted in the hospital. He is doing fine. He even told me where to find the key for his automobile." Singh held up a set of keys and shook them.

"Oh, my God, don't tell me that Ted is letting you drive his car."

"And why not? I learned to drive in Mumbai, with rickshaws and horse-drawn carriages and carts selling mangoes and taxis made out of bicycles and millions of beggars crossing the street in loin-cloths and turbans in between cows looking for food. If I can drive in that, I can drive anywhere."

They sat on the terrace and ate breakfast and discussed how exactly they were going to get rid of the Key.

"There's only one way this is going to work." Dalton sliced off a piece of a cantaloupe wedge, picked it up in his fingers, and took a bite. "The Vatican guys and the crazy Israelis have to believe that the Key is out of our possession."

Singh finished his eggs, set his knife and fork down beside his plate, took a bite out of a piece of toast, and jumped to his feet and began pushing things about the table as though he had lost something.

"What are you looking for?"

"Fresh chilies or spices, or something to sprinkle on this food to make it taste. How can people in America eat like this? There is no taste!"

"As soon as we get out of here, I'll buy you a bottle of curry powder that you can keep in your shirt pocket and sprinkle to your heart's content."

Singh shook his finger. "You are making fun of me, Mr. Dalton."

"Just Dalton; not 'Mr. Dalton.' I wouldn't make fun of you."

Air squished out of Singh's chair when he sat back down. After a moment he picked up a couple of the papers that Dalton had drawn a map on, along with notes. "And this is how we're going to get rid of the Key?"

"I've been planning it out in my head for a couple of days. Do you still have that shotgun?"

"I was hoping you were going to ask that, my friend. Yes, I have it, and I'm looking very much forward to blowing something up."

At the checkout counter in the lobby, the pretty young woman told Dalton that everything had already been taken care of.

"Give me the keys," said Dalton, holding out his hand as they crossed the lobby.

"Oh, no. Now it is Singh's turn to drive. This car that Mr. Ted has, it is a real car, a real American muscle car, not like that little skateboard rickshaw thing that the redheaded Nick drives. I just need to get used to this thing they call the clutch. I watched the video on YouTube about how to use it, but there's still this grinding sound when I change gears."

Dalton stopped. "You're kidding. Please, don't torture me like this. Just give me the keys."

Even before the car came around the corner with the valet behind the wheel, Dalton heard it coming, that low rumble of a V-8 Chevy with glass packs and a mild cam. It was what cars were supposed to sound like.

The valet revved the engine before he turned off the ignition.

Singh flipped the valet five dollars. The engine started easy enough with Singh behind the wheel, but then came the hard part, shifting into gear, getting the car to pull away from the curb. There was a bit of grinding, and the car lunged forward and stalled twice before the Indian got it rolling. By the time they made it to the freeway, Singh was shifting gears well. When he accelerated up the on-ramp, the car rose up off the pavement like a racehorse wanting to run.

"This isn't like driving a Toyota, Singh. If you step on the gas she's going to get up and take off. So be ready, and that means two hands on the fricking wheel."

"You are not my boss. What was it that Mr. Nick said to you? Oh, yes: if you don't like my car, you can take a taxi. I like that. That is a very American thing to say."

"Do you remember the way to Jax's apartment? You followed me there once."

Singh turned on his blinker and looked over his shoulder to change lanes, reached down and shoved the gear shift from fourth to third gear, and stomped on the gas. The Malibu shivered, and climbed up on its own wheels, and took off as Singh laughed.

"Look at me, Singh. Now this is really California cruising."

"This is embarrassing."

They drove slowly once they got off the freeway, through the side streets, turning this way and that, and finally made it onto Jax's street. They had only gone about twenty feet along the road when Dalton sat up straight and took off his seat belt and looked about.

"That's gunpowder I smell."

Up ahead there was a black Lincoln Town Car double-parked in the street with its emergency flashers blinking. The unmistakable sound of gunfire popped through the air. Dalton felt the repercussion of the shots on his face.

They were almost there when the front door of Jax's apartment crashed open. A man rushed out, turned and fired twice back into the building, and jumped out of the doorway. He cleared the door just-in-time. The loud, deep boom of shotgun fire came from within the building. The buckshot burst a hole through the door. The second shot blew off the top hinge and threw splinters of wood and paint into the street. The man ran to the Town Car, shouting, and jumped inside.

"Gregory," shouted Dalton, climbing halfway out of his window and firing four rounds into the back of the other car as it sped down the street.

"That was Jax's house," he shouted.

"Should I stop?" Singh glanced over.

"If I know my woman, she's good. Catch that bastard."

The big Lincoln ahead took the corner too fast and crashed into an old Datsun on milk crates. The crates shot out, and the Datsun fell. The Lincoln burned rubber in the street and sent a cloud of smoke behind it as it sped away.

"Hit that car, Singh. Crash into them." Dalton slapped the dashboard. "You got the power; use it!"

Singh downshifted and pressed the gas. Soon they were gaining on the car ahead. "But this is Mr. Ted's car. I don't want to hurt it."

"That was Jax's house. Ted would be the first one to use his car like a rocket and smash that guy off the road."

Singh nodded and whispered a little prayer. He let off the gas and shoved the transmission down into second gear, revved the engine until it sounded as though it was going to explode right out of the hood, and he dumped the clutch. The back wheels spun on the pavement, and the car turned sideways as it raced up the road at forty miles an hour. That's when Singh started screaming at the top of his lungs, as though he was scared out of his mind. But he wouldn't let off the throttle. He was almost right behind that black Town Car, shifting up and shifting down, from one gear to another, banging the shifts and stomping on the accelerator when he needed to, turning into each slide and whipping the wheel around every time the tires broke loose from the pavement.

Dalton shoved his hands against the ceiling, pressed his legs hard on the floorboard, grabbed his seatbelt and pulled it tight around his waist.

"My shotgun! Please get my little shotgun underneath the seat. I so badly want to shoot this brute."

Their quarry ran a stop sign and turned onto a main boulevard. Several cars locked up their brakes and skidded. One of the cars spun and jumped the curb into the glass doors of a shop.

People screamed and ran down the sidewalk, and hid behind parked cars.

Just as the Town Car turned a corner, Singh stomped on the accelerator and crashed into its rear quarter panel, pushing the back of the car sideways, and spinning it around.

For a split second the car stopped, dead even with the Malibu.

Dalton climbed up on his door with the shotgun and fired over the top of Ted's car, blowing out the window of the Lincoln. The glass shattered and fell into the street, and he got a clear view of Gregory whipping around with his weapon, about to fire. But the Malibu jumped forward and drove up the street until Singh locked up the brakes, shoved it into reverse, did a burnout up a driveway. Then he slammed the shifter back into first, and came after the Lincoln.

Dalton flipped open the shotgun and pulled out the spent shells, grabbed new ones from the glove compartment, and shoved them into the chambers. They were moving at sixty miles an hour down the boulevard, and Dalton had just finished loading the weapon, when a car came out of a side street and T-boned them. The Malibu hopped sideways about twenty feet and came to a stop in the road.

Singh shook his head and looked around.

In the second that they sat there motionless, Dalton looked over at the vehicle that hit them.

In the driver's seat sat Uri Dent.

He didn't even try to open his door, but climbed out the window and ran across the street. When he reached the other car, Dalton jumped up on the hood and fired two rounds straight through the windshield and into the driver. After firing the rounds, he wondered whether the guy was wearing a bulletproof vest, and fired another round through the driver's forehead.

When shots are fired in an urban area, a few moments of silence follow. It's when the residents, the people out walking, doing their shopping, those who slam on their brakes and flop down onto the passenger seat for safety, all pause and wonder if there is going to be more gunfire.

The city fell silent.

Dalton thought about Jax. The Town Car was heading toward Jax's place. He had to stop it. Dalton ran back to the Malibu and climbed in.

"Catch him again, Singh. I'm going to end this."

"It is a big car, that Lincoln." Singh twisted his hands on the steering wheel and leaned forward. "But my Malibu is faster." He dumped the clutch and smoked the tires; they raced down the road.

They slowed down at several small intersections so they could peer up and down the streets, looking for the car. Five or six streets up the boulevard, they spotted it.

"Get back to Jax's place! We're never going to catch him."

CHAPTER 25

Dalton jumped out of the car and ran down the street beside the parked cars. His lungs drew air in and out with hoarse gasps as he struggled to run faster, his arms pumping hard, feet hardly touching the asphalt. He heard that voice inside him that had so often come to him during missions in foreign countries, saying to run, get out of the way, go further, do more, fire back and save the men fighting beside him.

But now it was different. Jax was his every thought; he had to get to her. Gregory had come running out of her house. And he was sure something terrible had happened. For two years now, he had kept these memories of her laughing, touching him softly as they exchanged pillow talk. Was that gone? Was she lying in a pool of blood, moving boxes piled around her on the floor? Somehow, he realized, *this* was all for her. His hiding, changing his identity, going to her at night on the computer, looking through the yearbook to drum up memories, trying to make her real enough in his mind so he could touch her. All the cases he'd worked; it was all for Jax. Who would he be without her?

A woman opened her car door and Dalton slammed into it and shouted an apology as he spun around and rolled off the door. He sprinted away with the gun in his hand. Cars skidded to a halt around him. He kept pushing himself to go faster, ignoring the pain in his chest, and the burning in his throat.

The car came around the corner just as he was sprinting across the sidewalk and over the curb. Dalton couldn't avoid it. He jumped and slid across the hood, and landed headfirst in the street. He rolled a couple times, and then he was up again, his elbows bleeding, a scrape on the side of his face.

The front door of Jax's house stood open two inches, with a big shotgun hole in it. Dalton stopped outside, breathing loudly, panting, and did a rapid-fire look into the house, thrusting his head forward and pulling it back quickly before he got shot. Before he moved into the doorway, he pulled the door so that it closed slightly before him, and then he called in a loud, concerned voice: "Jax, are you in there? Are you okay?"

Gunfire erupted inside the house. The door exploded close to his face. The shot blew off the doorknob. Woodchips flew into the air, landing in his hair and peppering his face. The doorknob flew across the sidewalk, out into the street, and spun a few times before it stopped.

His ears rang. He looked at the door with disbelief. A big half circle was missing where a shotgun blast had hit. He didn't want to be anywhere near it when that cannon discharged again.

"It's Dalton! Jax, are you okay? It's me, don't shoot."

"Dalton!" she screamed.

A second later she was at the door and pulled it open. Her blonde hair was sticking out around her face. Bits of drywall and paint and woodchips thrown up by the gunfire clung to her hair and eyelashes. She was dressed like a painter in worn-out overalls and a man's checkered shirt with cut-off sleeves; the frayed threads hung down her arms.

She screamed and cried, and it was hard to understand what she was saying as she wrapped her arms around him and pulled him tight. But it wasn't all her that pressed against him. Between them was the hard steel of the shotgun.

"Whoa, okay, okay. Here, let me take that." Dalton pushed her away and took the shotgun out of her hand; he leaned it against the wall.

"Oh, my God, I was painting the back room and that Samoan

man grabbed me. I bit his arm and tore a piece of meat out of it and stopped on his foot like you taught me to do." She panted and cried and hit him on the shoulder.

"It's okay, babe. I'm here. We're going to stay together. No more running away to protect you."

"I didn't know what to do, Dalton. They were in my house! That ugly Samoan screamed when I bit him. Then I remembered that shotgun you bought."

Dalton pulled her out of the doorway. "Are there any more in there?"

"I killed that big man. I think I killed him, Dalton. And then I just started shooting, and Gregory started shooting back at me, and I shot and shot until he ran out the front door and I almost got him as he was running away." She burst into tears.

Dalton held her tightly against him as he walked through the apartment, the gun held out in front of him. Furniture had been knocked over. A table sat upside down on the floor with bits of drywall and dirt strewn across it. Round holes decorated the walls where the shotgun blasts had hit. He moved slowly through the living room, peeked into the kitchen, and started down the hall toward the bedroom. That's where he saw blood splatter on the wall.

"You stay out here, okay. I'm just gunna take a look. I'll be right back."

Jax nodded and pressed her back to the wall. She slid down onto the floor, where she sat all balled up, her face pressed against her knees as she cried.

It was there in the bedroom, the floor covered with a plastic drop cloth and taped to the baseboards, another drop cloth over the bed, the paint roller, ladder, and a pan full of paint sitting on the floor, that he found the driver. He lay on top of the paint can lid. His blood had mixed with the paint and flowed over the plastic. On his right forearm, the Samoan was missing a chunk of flesh.

Dalton put his gun away. He went and found Jax, sat beside her, and held her close. "It's all going to be okay."

In the distance he heard sirens. At the front door, a neighbor woman stepped into the house and looked around. "Oh, my God, what happened?"

Dalton did not turn to look. "I need you to step outside. This is a crime scene. The police are on the way."

"Jax," whispered Dalton, into her hair. "Why don't we get away from all this?"

She pulled away and looked in his eyes. "What are you saying?"

"I'm saying what I've always wanted. When this is all over, why don't you and me just fly away? We'll go somewhere nice, somewhere in the tropics, close to the ocean, and start a new life."

"I don't want to be left again."

"No, I'll never make that mistake again. Good or bad, we're in this together. I shouldn't have left you."

"All I want is you."

"Then that's what we're going to do." Sitting there against the wall, Dalton whispered in a frantic voice, and told her about his plan to end the case.

A siren sounded a few blocks away, and Dalton said, "I need you to get your phone. The police are going to be here in a moment. You need your lawyer here with you. I'm sure they are going to haul us both to the station for questioning."

Jax stood and brushed the tears from her cheeks, took a breath, and looked about. She rubbed her arm as though she was cold, brushed off her pants, and walked to the kitchen counter and picked up her cell phone.

* * *

The air conditioning in the police department made the room cold.

FBI agent Lowenthal shouted, "I have three witnesses that

say you jumped on the hood of that car right there in that photo, and killed the driver with three shots. I also have blood samples and bullets from your gun that prove you killed the man."

Mr. Steinberg, a round little bald man who wore spectacles on the end of his nose, jumped to his feet and slapped the table. "You don't have a body. If you don't have a body, you can't charge my client with a crime. Mr. Dalton and I have better things to do than sit here and be subjected to FBI rantings and ravings about blood and bullets. My client is not being charged with a crime, gentlemen. Good day to you." Mr. Steinberg stood and kicked over his chair and tugged on Dalton's shoulder.

Dalton stood up and looked around the room. "You lost a body? I'll bet your boss wishes his jaw wasn't wired shut so he could shout at you."

Dalton pulled on his blazer and walked out of the interrogation room.

Special Agent Lowenthal followed him into the corridor. "I think your friends over there want to speak to you, Dalton."

He followed Lowenthal's gesture. At the end of the hall, standing in the waiting room, were two buff young men that he had seen before. Between them stood Commander Rossi, his arms crossed on his chest, his hand tapping a hundred miles an hour on his arm.

Lowenthal leaned forward and whispered, "When we got to the scene of the shooting, they were there. Two of them were covered with blood as though they'd carried a body, but we couldn't touch them because they have diplomatic passports. Ain't that a bitch? Now they're just hanging around the police station, waiting for your ass to get out."

Dalton approached the three men. "What do you want, Rossi?"

"I should've kept a closer eye on Dent. It seems he had his own agenda. That organization that helped Devonshire get those paintings out of Europe, also hired Uri Dent. They're out there, Dalton, and they know about you. We took Dent's body away as a professional courtesy. Now I'm giving you a heads up.

Careful in the shadows. I'm here to tell you that whatever they have planned for you, I have nothing to do with it."

"Listen, Rossi, I'm tired. I want to get rid of the Key. Why don't you meet me on top of the Long Beach Yacht Club? Beside the jetty, at two o'clock tomorrow afternoon? Meet me there, and I'll turn it over to you."

The commander raised his chin as though he was trying to decide whether he believed the man before him. "Why would you do that?"

"That thing's not doing me any good, okay? People have been trying to kill me ever since I looked at it. My client doesn't want it because it ties her to the illegal dealings of her husband. And me? I just want to live a normal life, without all this, okay?"

"Tomorrow at two o'clock." The commander nodded.

"I'm trying to do the right thing."

* * *

It didn't take Jax's lawyer very long before she was free. After all, the intruder had broken into her house and assaulted her. She had defended herself in her home, and the suspect had died. The Somoan had a record, and that supported Jax's story. There would be no charges.

Dalton wrapped Jax in his blazer the second she came out of the interrogation room. He led her down the hall, and after a few words with the lawyer, they left the police station.

CHAPTER 26

On the way back, Singh drove while Dalton sat in the back with Jax.

While they were driving, Jax's phone rang. She spoke for a couple of minutes, and put the cell back in her purse. "It was a nurse in the hospital. He said that Ted left."

"Have you spoken to him today?"

"For a little while."

"You didn't mention the shooting, did you?"

The smile disappeared from Jax's face, and she looked down. "He knew that something happened. He heard it in my voice. I'm not good at hiding things like that."

"You told him it was Gregory?"

"Gregory and his driver, yes. I told him."

Dalton reached over and placed a hand on top of hers. "You know he's going to protect you, right?"

Jax nodded her head. "That's what he does for his family. Ever since high school, Ted's been watching out for me. Even when you went away and played dead, Ted was always coming by and helping out, giving me pep talks to keep me going, getting me back into school."

Dalton laughed and shook his head. He looked out at the traffic. "The guy's lying in a hospital bed and hears you were in a shooting. So, he checks himself out and goes to play big brother. I feel sorry for Gregory."

"I don't know if he can thump anybody. The nurse said he took a wheelchair, so he's not walking too well."

"That doesn't matter. Last mission Ted and I served together, he was more dangerous after he got wounded than he was before. Maybe it was just a flesh wound, but it made him angry and mean. Crap. He considers you family, and he thinks somebody's out to get his family."

Jax laid her head on Dalton's shoulder. "I wish we could get this over with."

"That's what we're doing."

* * *

They entered Dalton's building from the parking lot and walked up the old marble staircase. On the landing they crowded together as Dalton played with the key in the lock, trying to get the door open. Just as it clicked, he saw movement through the new glass, and he froze.

"Singh, where is your gun?" he whispered.

Singh reached beneath his jacket and pulled out the sawed-off shotgun. He took a breath as though he was about to explain why he'd bought the shotgun…and about his family in India and how he cooked rice as well.

But Jax covered his mouth with her hand, and pointed into the office.

Holding his hand in the air and raising one finger at a time Dalton counted silently, one, two, and opened the door.

Singh ran into the office with the shotgun held out in front of him.

"Whoa!" shouted Nick. "It's me. Don't shoot."

"I'm glad you're back." Dalton shook his hand and pulled him forward, and they embraced.

"I'm glad to be back," said Nick. "And this must be Jax. It's about time you two got together. I've been reading all about you for months now, trying to talk some sense into this fool, trying to get him to knock on your door." He stepped around Dalton, took Jax's hand in his own, and they spoke for a few minutes.

"A lot has happened since you left," Dalton said.

Nick pushed his hair back. "I'll bet it has, Boss. I've been following along as much as I could with e-mails from my computer buddies. They've been telling me as much as they know about what's going on. Is it true that Sophie Devonshire hung you out to dry? A fingerprint, is that all they have? We wiped that place down two or three times. There's no way we left a fingerprint behind."

"Yeah, but I sent in the Italian special forces. That's their specialty. They could've planted a fingerprint. That's what they do."

Dalton sat down in the creaking desk chair. He pulled the Velcro loose on his shoulder holster, and set his weapon on the desk. "So, tell me about Texas."

"Yeah, good old Sophie Devonshire is not who she pretends to be. I got birth certificates and everything to prove it. We have a lot of leverage."

"You have all the paperwork with you?"

"I have paperwork and digital recordings of the interviews I did with witnesses. These are people that knew them both, neighbors and schoolmates. Remember what I told you about that birthmark?"

"Yeah, and our client definitely has one."

Dalton walked around the desk and sat down in front of Nick. "And you still have what we took out of the basement, right?"

"It's safe. I got it stashed away where no one is going to find it."

"Good. Keep it that way."

"But who is getting hungry?" asked Singh from across the office, banging some pots and pans in the corner.

"And you're still here in the country?" Nick walked over to Singh's cooking area.

"Singh is a regular gangster now." Dalton laughed. "The guy

carries a sawed-off shotgun and drives like a maniac."

"Oh, Mr. Nick, you should have seen me driving Ted's Malibu. That is a real car, with a four-speed transmission, and a big V-8 engine. American muscle."

"No! Did Ted let him drive the Malibu?"

"He did more than drive. He ground a few pounds of gears in the transmission trying to figure out how to use the clutch, but he did good. Singh laid rubber like you wouldn't believe. He saved us."

"Saved you?" asked Nick.

"Oh, you haven't heard?"

Jax picked up a blanket from the sofa and wrapped it around her shoulders. "I hired a man named Gregory to find Dalton. But something went wrong. Maybe that artifact thing made him want more money."

Dalton placed his hand on her shoulder. "She had to defend herself. Gregory's driver was killed."

"I'm sorry," said Nick.

Dalton clapped him on the shoulder as he passed. "We're doing this thing tomorrow. I need to know who's going to come along. Singh and I have arranged a little exchange."

"Exchange for what?" Nick looked around.

"I'm exchanging Solomon's Key for our freedom. They get the Key, and we get to walk away knowing they're not chasing us. I'm getting real tired of looking over my shoulder every time I step through a door or turn a corner. I want this to be finished."

"We all want that, don't we?" Jax looked around the room.

"The only way you're going to finish it is to hand over the Key. Then we all have to disappear."

Dalton walked over to the white board. "Exactly. We don't know if they're going treasure hunting with the Key map, or what they're going to do with it. But I'm more than certain they don't want anybody talking about it. So that means we have to disappear for a while. Is everyone good with that?"

"That is fine with me. I will be happy to be back in India. I have missed my temple. I will take time to be there every single day, after I take care of my sick mother. That is where I will be, in the temple, praying." Singh took a deep breath that everyone in the room heard.

"Me? I'm good. As long as I got an Internet connection, I'll be good wherever I'm at. Maybe I'll go down to that little village in Mexico that you're always talking about, Boss."

"Good," said Dalton, turning to the white board. "Let me show you the plan. Singh, is everything ready to go with your brother-in-law?"

Singh shut off the water and wiped the inside of a pot with a dishtowel. "Yes, Dalton. He assured me today that the product is just perfect, and ready to go."

"That's all I needed to know. The only thing we can't control is Gregory. I invited the Vatican soldiers to be there so I could turn the Key over to them. That means the Israelis will probably be following them to the trade. What happens with Gregory is out of my control, but you guys have to be ready for anything. So, here's the way I see it going down."

Dalton drew on the whiteboard and explained the location and the times, and exactly how he saw the trade unfolding. For more than half an hour he answered questions and explained where each member of the team was going to be.

When everybody seemed content about their part in the transaction, they took the cushions off the sofa, and laid them about the office floor as beds. One by one they stretched out and tried to sleep.

CHAPTER 27

Just after six that morning, Dalton smelled bacon and curry. He rolled over on the uncomfortable cushion from the sofa, and pulled Jax close. It felt good having her there, being able to touch her, feel the soft curve of her hip beneath his hand. He opened his eyes and looked at her sleeping face.

The smells from Singh's cooking drew his attention to the corner, where the Indian man with the soft middle was humming a song as he stirred a pot in his makeshift kitchen.

Dalton stood up and walked over. "Singh, where in a bacon-and-eggs breakfast does curry powder fit in?"

"Good morning." Singh held up a letter opener that he had been stirring with.

"Why are you using my letter opener? Never mind."

"I wish they could build a trash truck that was quieter." Nick closed the office door behind him with his foot as he balanced two Starbucks carry trays. He went over and set them on the desk.

"Everyone, check your weapons before we leave. Make sure you have plenty of ammo. I don't think there's going to be gunfire, but it's best to be prepared." Dalton picked up one of the plates of food, reached down and returned a cushion to the sofa. Then he sat and ate.

The city was waking up. There was a cold chill in the air, a California chill. That meant the temperature had dropped into the forties during the night. One or two cars drove slowly down the street. Behind the wheel of one, Dalton saw the driver sipping from a travel mug.

"Okay, everybody! Singh is going to the airport."

Nick and Jax and Dalton joked with Singh as they followed him out of the office, down the stairs, and out onto the sidewalk. There was an awkward silence as they stood on the corner waiting for the taxi. During that time of waiting, Dalton leaned over and glanced around the corner of his building, toward the approaching trash truck. He nodded to a morning jogger coming toward him, then watched as the woman turned the corner and side-stepped around Singh and the others.

"Why are you looking so nervous," asked Nick.

"We're standing on a corner. I can't watch the street in front of us and around the corner at the same time." Dalton shook his head.

Jax rushed over and pulled Nick and Dalton to the curb beside Singh's bags as the taxi pulled up.

They patted Singh on the back and told him to have a good trip. Nick mentioned something about their wild ride on Signal Hill, and the Volkswagen, and they laughed.

"Remember what I told you, Singh," said Dalton. "Buy a few souvenirs and stuff them in the same bag. That way, if they open the bag when you arrive in India, it'll look like a cheap souvenir. You do have it, right?"

"Yes, Mr. Dalton. Stop worrying. I have the Key."

And you called your brother-in-law, right? He's knows I'm coming to pick up our copy?"

Singh did the head-bob thing. "Yes, he knows. We've been over this and over this. Now all you have to do is drive over there and pick it up and everything is done. We all go on our own way now. You've done a fine job of planning this."

The taxi driver climbed out and opened the back door of his car, and Singh drove away, waving in the rear window.

Dalton waved until the sound of a struggle made him turn.

Gregory must have walked around the corner of the building

while everyone was saying goodbye to Singh. Major Gregory had his arm wrapped around Jax's neck, and was dragging her to the corner, a pistol against her ear.

Nick dropped his coffee and reached beneath his jacket for his weapon.

"No, Nick!" Dalton grabbed his arm. He stood there as Gregory pulled Jax a few more feet, and stopped.

"Don't let him get around the corner," whispered Nick.

Dalton took a half step forward.

"He's going to put her in a car. Stop him."

Dalton reached toward her, wanting to pull her back, to touch Jax, touch the memories and protect her. But all he could touch was cold air.

Jax struggled and fought, twisted and threw her elbow into the assailant's ribs, but Gregory knew all the tricks. He was much too big and strong.

"I know you have it, Dalton. Give it to me now and I'll let her go."

"What are you talking about? Just let her go, Gregory. This is between me and you."

Nick took a step into the street.

"Stop! I will not be flanked." Gregory pulled back the trigger and cocked the weapon. Only a slight twitch of his finger, and Jax's head would explode. "I know you have Solomon's Key. It's worth millions. Give it to me, or lose her."

"I don't have it with me."

"Then we have a serious problem, Mr. Dalton. Say goodbye to your woman." Gregory stepped away from Jax and extended his arm straight, the gun against her temple.

"Wait a minute. Don't do this. Don't take her away from me again, please. I'll get it for you. I know where it is. All I have to do is drive over there and get it. I'm begging you, please don't do this."

As Dalton spoke he saw a wheelchair come slowly around the corner of the building behind Gregory. He tried not to let the expression on his face change, or Gregory would know that something was behind him, and turn and shoot.

Ted rolled forward until he was about four feet behind Gregory. Slowly he locked the wheels into place, and picked up the pillow in his lap. Bits of foam and cloth silently burst from the pillow and fell to the sidewalk as Ted fired his pistol.

"Oh," said Gregory, as though choking. He dropped to his knees. The weapon in his hand fell to the pavement.

"You messed with my family," said Ted. "I thought everyone around the city knew better than to mess with Ted's family. A big bad man like you, you sneak into a woman's home and attack her? Now look at you, down on your knees, looking at the world for the last time."

He fired again, and Gregory fell face down. His head thumped against the sidewalk.

Ted rolled his wheelchair to the curb, glanced at the approaching trash truck, and tossed his pistol into a trash can. "I'm guessing you guys have some business to take care of. Like right now."

Jax ran over and wrapped her arms around Ted. "You came to save me, Ted. You've been saving me ever since high school."

Ted laughed and patted her arm. "I saved you because that was my promise to Dalton, a soldier's promise. He had to go away to save you. I told him I'd look after you."

"And that's what you did." Dalton extended his hand to the man in the wheelchair. "You gunna be okay?"

"Go now, you guys. You got a dead body on the sidewalk. There's no need for you to be around here." Ted rolled down the sidewalk. When he was twenty feet away, he turned. "I'm heading to the hood. I got a lady down there that used to be a nurse. She'll take care of me good."

Gregory's attempt to get the Key had cost them time. Dalton knew they had to move fast. The first stop they made was in Little India, where he picked up the copy of Solomon's Key. Looking at it, he had to admit that Singh had been right: his brother-in-law made a pretty good copy. Now all he had to do was make Rossi believe it was the real thing.

Nick was playing with the assault rifle the entire drive. "Are you sure this thing still fires?"

"It still fires," said Dalton. "If you want, I'll shoot one of those beanbags at you."

"Oh, hell, no. I don't need to be reminded."

* * *

There's a jetty that separates Seal Beach from Long Beach. On the Long Beach side, the suburb that backs up to that jetty is one of the most exclusive areas of the city. The houses on that long peninsula, wedged between Alamitos Bay and the Pacific, sell for over seven figures.

At the end of the long street to the jetty, sits the old yacht club building. Dalton pulled up beside the club and searched for a parking spot. They walked along the sidewalk, up the pathway bordered by ivy, and continued up the side of the staircase to the roof. It vibrated as they climbed.

Dalton smelled the ocean and felt a stiff breeze the moment he stepped onto the roof. Just over the side, less than ten feet away, were the jetty and the swift-flowing black ocean. Sailboats bounced over the swells. A few fishermen stood on the rocks, moving their poles up and down.

"Don't get too close to the edge," said Dalton, pulling Nick away.

"How do we know they're going to show?"

"Because I have the one thing they want most. And neither the Italians nor the Israelis want to risk the other getting it. They'll be here."

"I love this bulletproof vest, but man, it really makes me itch." Nick reached under his coat and scratched.

"Jax, you and Nick, you're stationed at the top of the staircase. There's no other way onto the roof. All you have to do is hold your ground. Make sure nobody else gets up the staircase. Allow the commander up, and then close it."

"How many times you gunna tell us that, Boss?"

"As many times as it takes to sink in. We're standing up here in the wind, with nowhere to go, no escape, so you best be sure you know what we're doing. We all want to walk away from this. Got it?"

"They're here!" shouted Jax, waving a hand.

Nick ran over and took position beside her. He leaned forward with the assault rifle, and pointed it down the staircase. "Only the commander!" he shouted.

Commander Rossi stepped onto the roof. When he saw Dalton, he walked to him. "You are not asking for money? All you want is my assurance that we will stop pursuing you. Is that correct?"

"You take Solomon's Key and walk away. That's the deal."

"And you have the Key with you?"

The sound of gunfire rang through the air. Several shots hit the edge of the rooftop and threw debris on the roof. Men shouted in the distance. A car skidded to a halt.

"It's the Israelis," shouted Nick, moving from the edge of the rooftop and peeking over the side.

"Hold the staircase. Don't let anyone up!" shouted Dalton.

Commander Rossi tapped the telephone in his ear and spoke. A moment later a shot knocked Nick off his feet.

Nick hit the rooftop face down, rolled, and moaned.

"Sniper!" shouted Dalton. He stepped sideways quickly and looked at Nick.

Although Nick was laying on the ground, Dalton didn't see any blood. He knew the shot must have hit the vest. He might have a broken rib, or a bruise that was going to last two weeks and hurt like hell, but he was alive.

Jax shouted and fired twice down the staircase. "They're trying to come up!"

More gunfire sounded on the street. Dalton heard an engine race, and the sound of two cars crashing together. Glass broke and scattered over the street.

"Let us conclude our business," shouted Rossi.

"Jax, get down, there's a sniper on that roof." Dalton ran toward her and motioned with his hands for her to lie down.

She dropped to her knees and then onto her belly, crawled forward and looked over the edge, and fired a couple of shots onto the staircase.

Dalton marched over and hit the commander on the shoulder. "Stop this! Nobody has to die here."

"Then hand over the artifact. Put Solomon's Key in my hand, and we'll be happy. I only need to speak one word into my telephone, and all this will stop."

Nick climbed to his feet, staggered forward, and fired the assault rifle.

The first bean bag hit the commander in the back of his knee, and dropped him to the rooftop. The second shot hit Dalton in the shoulder and spun him around.

"Give me the Key," shouted Nick. "Give it to me now, or I'll kill you both!"

A sniper's bullet whizzed by Dalton's face and grazed his cheek.

"Nick, what the hell are you doing?"

"I'm doing what I should've done days ago. Give it to me. That thing is worth millions. I'm tired of making peanuts. That money is mine now."

"I can't stop them," shouted Jax, ejecting the clip from her automatic, shoving another one into the handle. "They're too well armed! There's too many."

Dalton reached into his coat and pulled out the Key.

Commander Rossi said something and grabbed the artifact. His mouth fell open as he stared. "Solomon's treasure," he said in awe.

Dalton jerked it out of his hand.

"If you want it so bad, here it is." He held Solomon's Key out as he walked toward Nick. When he was five feet away, Dalton shouted and threw the artifact, ran and jumped over the side of the building. He wasn't in the air for more than a second before he hit the water. Even as he swam, he watched Commander

Rossi on the edge of the roof, shouting into the phone.

* * *

The secretary rushed into Sophie Devonshire's office. "You have two interviewees waiting in the lobby, Ms. Devonshire." She sat a stack of mail on the desk.

"Thank you, Louise. I'll be down to get the first one shortly." Sophie sorted through the mail and pulled out a brown envelope that looked interesting. With her gold letter opener, she cut open the envelope and poured several documents and photos onto her class-topped desk.

Among the notarized documents, the birth certificate, the photos of Sophie Devonshire and her teenage friend, she found a letter, and read:

This is the case I have built against you. Here you will find records that prove that Sophie Devonshire died in 2005. You'll also find notarized statements from neighbors and schoolmates who mentioned a particular birthmark on the left wrist of Sophie Devonshire's best friend, Sadie Crawford. That means that whoever is reading this letter is not Sophie Devonshire. If the case against Jason Dalton is not dropped, other copies of this evidence will be sent to the FBI, where a certain lieutenant will be very interested in the contents.

Sophie leaned back into her chair and stared at the ceiling. She stayed like that for more than five minutes, then picked up the phone and pressed her attorney's number.

* * *

Ted stretched out on the masseuse table and laughed. Through the circular hole where his face rested, through which he often drooled, he could see the shapely ankles of a woman as she worked his shoulders, and occasionally reached for a warm rock that she placed along his spine.

When the doorbell rang, Molly stopped the massage and hurried across Ted's loft to the front door.

He climbed up on the table as Molly was speaking to a deliveryman through the door.

"He won't leave the package, Honey."

Ted kissed her on the back of her neck, and gently pulled her away from the door. "I'll take care of it, Baby." He reached over and picked up the 9-mm door gun.

"Who is there?" he asked.

"This is FedEx. I have a delivery for Ted Martin."

"Just leave it on the porch."

"I have to get a signature. I cannot leave it. But if you refuse delivery, I'll take it back to the depot, and you could come and retrieve it later."

"Okay, I'll take it." Ted opened the door, shoving the gun into the crack as soon as it parted from the frame. Over the top of the weapon he saw the delivery driver's uniform, and pulled the door open.

He carried the package across the loft to the kitchen area, where he sat at the wooden picnic table and tore open the paper wrapping. As soon as he saw a bit of color, he jerked his head away as though he'd been slapped. "Holy crap," he whispered. He stuck his finger inside the package and touched a stack of crisp hundred-dollar bills. Then he lifted the package, about the size of a home printer, set it back down on the table, and pounded with his fist to see if it felt the same everywhere. It did.

The package was nothing but banded hundred-dollar bills. He tore a little more of the paper off. There, inside the package, on top of the bills, sat a map.

Ted pulled out the map and looked at it. Down toward the southern part of Mexico, was a circle drawn around the name of a town.

"I believe it's the rainy season in Honduras," he whispered, and laughed.

*   *   *

They waited at the border and watched men and women and families cross over the walking bridge between the United States and Mexico. Dalton hunched his shoulders under the weight of the new backpack.

Nick kept his hand on the top of his backpack at his feet.

Only Jax's backpack was not black. Hers was made of a flowered fabric. Every other detail—size, number of pockets, design—was the same as the black ones.

"I think it's best if we don't cross together."

"I'll go first," said Jax with a big smile, rocking onto her tiptoes.

"How's that rib of yours, Nick? Can you carry your pack?"

Nick nodded and swept his hair back. "Yeah, I'm good. It hurts like hell, but I'm not gunna set down my money."

Dalton rubbed his shoulder. "That bean bag shot to my shoulder hurts like hell, too."

"It was your plan." Nicked laughed.

Dalton chuckled, and said, "It was the only way I could think of to get the Key out of Rossi's hands, and it worked. Anyway, if we get separated, we'll meet in that little town."

"Okay," said Jax. "I'm going." She waved and repositioned the pack, then stepped into the flow of pedestrians heading for the border.

"How long do you think they're going to be looking for us?"

"I think the Vatican guys will be searching that jetty for a long time. And that's just the way I wanted it."

Nick chuckled and lifted the backpack. "When we Skyped with Singh, it was hanging on the wall of the Temple behind him. It was just hanging there with a hundred other relics."

"Hiding in plain sight, that's the best way. And Sophie Devonshire changed her story, so I don't have to worry about prosecution. Now it's only that organization I have to think about." Dalton started walking.

Nick hurried after him and grabbed his arm. "What are you talking about?"

"The organization that Devonshire ran. His henchmen are only interested in the cash. And we have it. It was only a matter of time before somebody came." Dalton took an embossed business card from his shirt pocket.

Nick read the card and turned it over. On the back was a handwritten note that said: *We would much appreciate the return of our property.*

"What do we do?"

"Well," said Dalton. "I'm going to the tropics to enjoy life. Legally, I believe Sophie Devonshire owns the money, and she doesn't want it. So, I'm going to have fun with Jax, and keep looking over my shoulder."

Dalton lifted his pack and walked across the bridge, into another country.

Nick followed a few minutes later.

The End

REVIEWS:

Dear reader, please help others make an informed choice about this book. Your review on Amazon will help. https://www.amazon.com/dp/B078MCJZ6Z#customerReviews

Thank you.
K.R. Hill

Made in the USA
Monee, IL
10 July 2022